MW01246077

HOPE
IS IT ON
TIME

CURTIS R. CREED

WESTBOW
PRESS®
A DIVISION OF THOMAS NELSON
& ZONDERVAN

WestBow Press books may be ordered through booksellers or by contacting:

WestBow Press
A Division of Thomas Nelson & Zondervan
1663 Liberty Drive
Bloomington, IN 47403
www.westbowpress.com
844-714-3454

Holy Bible, New International Version®, NIV® Copyright ©1973, 1978, 1984,
2011 by Biblica, Inc.® Used by permission. All rights reserved worldwide.

ISBN: 979-8-3850-2666-1 (sc)
ISBN: 979-8-3850-2667-8 (hc)
ISBN: 979-8-3850-2668-5 (e)

Library of Congress Control Number: 2024911001

Print information available on the last page.

WestBow Press rev. date: 8/22/2024

CONTENTS

Prologue 1

Did It Finally Arrive? 5

The Birth 12

Christian Returns 23

The Truth Comes Out 29

Survival: Fight or Flight 37

A Community Begins to Grow 47

One More Round 58

Secrets Cannot Be Kept 67

Bad News for Brutus 78

Strength Is Here 86

Time to Get Ready 98

The Time Has Come 111

PROLOGUE

L ife had been so simple in the large community until gold was found. Sitting on top of a low cliff overlooking the ocean was the village of Kyrre, which consisted mostly of miners, carpenters, stonecutters, and blacksmiths. In it was a single monastery that cared for the people. The blacksmiths made items out of the copper and iron that were mined. Stonecutters made things out of marble and buildings out of granite and sandstone. Carpenters built items as well. Farmers grew food to feed the population. All the craftsmen sent their wares to Svantovit for trade and to pay tribute to King Archibald. The people did not mind paying tribute to the king. Though he was far away, they were safe and happy.

The people were masters of their trades and used their skills to make a beautiful way of life. They made elegant one- and two-story stone houses and cobblestone roads. They incorporated nature in all their work. They built parks and filled them with natural flowers and trees where the workers and their families could enjoy restful time after working a hard day. The smell of the flowers was serene. The children would run about as the parents would rest under the shade.

In the two-story houses, people set up shops on the lower floors where they sold tools, crafts, and food. Every morning the smell of fresh pastries being baked filled the air around the baker's shop.

The people were thankful for what they had. They noticed that the monastery was a in disrepair, so they decided to build an angelic chapel in the center to thank God for the blessings they had been given. It took years to build the chapel, but it was a masterpiece with decorative windows, pews, columns, statues, and other features. They built a separate building where the monks could live. Once the chapel was completed, people attended services to thank God.

Word got out how wonderful life was in Kyrre, and more people came. More farms were developed where new farmers grew food to feed the people. Everything was picturesque and peaceful. It was a safe place to raise a family. Everyone worked together and respected each other. They enjoyed the view from the cliff looking over the ocean so much that they set aside a field there where families could gather. Stonecutters cut stairs into the side of the cliff so the people could walk down to the beach below. From the ocean side there were two ways into the town —these stairs or a road at the end of the cliff 550 feet down the coast.

One day, a miner found some gold. Two of the monks heard about it and wanted some to decorate the new chapel that had just been built. It was not too long until the king himself heard about it as well. The king asked for some in tribute, but he received little. The two monks liked the way the gold looked in their new chapel and wanted more for the chapel and themselves. The tribute to the king became smaller. The king asked again for more in tribute, and again did not receive much because it was the monks who were in charge of sending tribute to the king. One night, one of the monks had a dream that a child with a birthmark would save the community. He did not think much of it, but he told the other monks about it. No one thought their tranquility would be shattered.

One day, three ships showed up in the community's port. The king had arrived! The king decided to go to the chapel. There he discovered all the items made from gold. The two monks argued with the king because their love for gold was great. The king then decided to have all the monks killed. But he would leave the people of the community alone for it was not their fault. In the monastery, three young monks—Samuel, Benjamin, and Paul—saw what was going on. They ran to a false wall in the monastery, slid it open, and entered a secret room where they stayed until it was safe to come out. The three monks then escaped through a tunnel that led from the monastery into a gulley and ran into the woods. They waited for several months in the woods until the hair had grown back in their tonsures. During this time, they received aid from the villagers. When the three monks no longer looked like monks, the villagers invited them to join them.

Samuel was the most devoted to God and had a love for the land. He loved watching things grow from good soil. Paul loved to cook and make meals for their community. For those who needed help, he would provide meals. Benjamin was a little different and feeble. Being a monk was not his first choice. He was good with animals and enjoyed taking care of them.

When they returned, their beloved community was being changed by King William, a puppet king to King Archibald who was in control of sending tributes. Right away, King William ordered the people to build walls around the community. The walls were twenty-five feet tall and fifteen feet thick of stone and ashlar. The king ordered the building of two barracks, stables, and a running yard for the horses. The village scenic overlook became a castle. It was set close to the cliff with many windows on the cliff side. One could say that King William was making Kyrre safe from ever being sieged. Outside the walls, huts were constructed for the newer families. These replaced the stone houses previously set aside for workers and their families. Nothing was nice about the huts outside the castle wall.

Soon King William did not care much about the villagers. He took what he wanted from them. The soldiers who were in his service did the same. No one challenged them because they weren't sure how. They had never had to fight. They could not leave because the king controlled them, and the soldiers did his bidding. The king turned the monastery into a dungeon. Anyone who challenged the king was thrown into the dungeon. When the king wanted to make an example of someone, that person was put into the new pillory in the courtyard in front of the castle so everyone could see.

For so many years, the village of Kyrre had been a utopia, but all of that ended when greed came to only a few who did not follow the teachings of the villagers.

So, the monks, Samuel, Benjamin, and Paul told the people one of the head monks had once had a dream, and they told them about the dream: A child with a birthmark would come to save them. They did this to give their people some hope—hope to carry on, for there was no more happiness in the way they were living. The dream seemed like a fable to most people, but it gave hope to others.

DID IT FINALLY
ARRIVE?

A voice called out in the night, "Where are you taking me?" "Hush up! No one wants to hear you speak," Brutus, one of the soldiers, yelled.

"Where are you taking me?" the person asked again.

"Take him to the castle courtyard and throw him into the pillory," Brutus replied with a smile, for he was going to enjoy this.

All that could be heard was the chains clanging as the group walked down the cobblestone road. Finally, they reached the courtyard, which was lit by torches.

"Put him in it and secure him," Brutus commanded. Soldiers placed the man's arms and neck into the pillory and applied the chains.

"Rip off the back of his shirt," Brutus directed. A soldier ripped the back of the man's shirt while Brutus looked around. His eyes fixated on a whip that was on a carriage near them. "Grab that whip and use it!" Brutus directed, and then he looked at the man in chains.

As ordered, another soldier retrieved the whip and started hitting the man in the pillory. There was no other sound in the night but the cracking of the whip as it dug into his skin. The man did not ask for mercy or give them the satisfaction of crying out in pain. All he said was, "You do not need to do this."

The soldier continued to whip the man. The whip dug into his skin leaving a deep, long, and bloodied slashes on his bare back.

Brutus was starting to enjoy this. He replied, "Oh, on the contrary, I do need to do this. Don't worry. I am going to keep you alive. Make you an example. You can rest, for I am not going to make you a martyr. I just liked the way things were before, but this time I am in charge."

Some of the soldiers laughed.

"Don't stop your punishment!" Brutus commanded with no remorse or mercy in his accented tone. The soldier with the whip gave the man two more strikes, the whip digging deep into the man's skin. Blood dripped onto the ground from the end of the whip. Finally, Brutus put up his hand, signaling the soldier to stop.

The man just stared at Brutus, not showing any sign of weakness, but definitely showing a desire to react.

Brutus looked back at him and said, "I can see the anger in your eyes. That is good. There is one thing I do not understand. You were nicknamed Hope because people believed you could save them. You were also given the name Christian. It is time for you to realize, Christian, that you are no one's hope." Brutus took one step closer so he towered over Christian. He could see that Christian was wearing only one wristband on his right hand. Brutus reached out to touch it and said, "Let's see which one you have on your wrist." Brutus lifted it up and read aloud. "'Love God.' Did you not have another one? What was it now? 'God loves you'? You must have given up on that." Brutus laughed a little. "What, did you realize he does not love you, so you got rid of it? How could a merciful God let you come into my hands? Wait, are you going to tell me he has a plan?" Brutus chuckled. "You know, it was a good thing for King William to order the people get rid of their Bibles. By denying them the scriptures, he took faith and hope away from them. I have seen religion have a powerful influence, but when there is none, I have noticed the people seem to be more manageable." Brutus stood up straight. "We'll be back in the morning to make sure everyone is here to watch." He smiled menacingly. "Once they see you break, they will not dare to challenge me again."

"You have planned this well out, haven't you?" Christian replied.

"I have waited years to take advantage of a situation like this that could make me king! Who would have figured the person people call Hope would help me take over? Wait, you were my hope as well!" Brutus chuckled but then regained his calm. "So you know I was part of William's plan to kill your family. You were supposed to die with them, but somehow you got out and were saved. Now, because I will keep you alive, you will help me put fear into the hearts of the people and give me full control. You can no longer offer the people the hope of freedom!"

Christian stared at Brutus with utmost hatred. "Why don't you give me a sword? I will fight all of you, Brutus. I know you are still scared of me."

Brutus chuckled and smirked at him. "You are a dangerous man, but that is why you will stay in chains. I do not want to take the chance of damaging you just yet. You are the best tool for keeping everyone in line, Hope." Brutus looked at the soldiers. "We are done talking. Take him to the dungeon. Take him to the old man and tell him to dress his wounds. We don't want him to die just yet." He turned to Christian. "In the morning, Hope, we will put on a show for the people, but I promise that you will barely be able to walk after we are done."

As a small group of soldiers took Christian away, Christian looked back and yelled, "You are a coward, Brutus."

"But I am the one in charge." And Brutus walked away.

Christian struggled to get out of his restraints, but the soldiers did not give him a chance. Once they got to the dungeon, they opened a cell and threw him down on the ground with his chains still on. He landed next to an old man.

One of the guards said, "Ben, here is someone to join you. He may need your help. Take care of the wounds on his back. We will be back for him in the morning." Then the soldiers left.

Ben looked at Christian but could not see much. He then felt the newcomer's back and found that it was wet. Ben realized it was blood and began tending to his wounds. Ben said, "This might hurt. Tell me your name, kid."

Christian avoided showing any sign of pain. "My name is Christian."

Ben looked confused. "I do not remember that name. Even though I am in here, I do hear of things that happen outside." Ben's face started to change as if he was going into shock. He moved Christian's hair slightly to the side so he could look at his face. "Where are you from?"

"I am from here. I was raised by King William after my parents were murdered by his soldiers at his direction." Christian stalled and took a breath. "People sometimes call me Hope."

Ben looked up at the ceiling and started to cry. An immense guilt rose inside him. He could hardly do anything, so he said, "Please help me, God." Tears ran down his face as he cleaned and dressed Hope's wounds.

Morning came, and the soldiers came to get Christian. They unlocked the cell door, but Ben jumped right in front of the soldiers. "He is not ready," Ben said.

The soldiers knocked Ben down and beat him. Right then, Christian got up and started to wrestle with the soldiers. As he grabbed one around the neck, he noticed that the soldiers did not carry any weapons. One soldier closed the cell door. Another soldier, standing in a dark corner, said to him, "So, Hope, are you going to let him go? Tell me, do you have a plan?" The man's voice was familiar to Hope.

"Carl, I should have known you were involved in this. It is nice to see that scar on your face is still there," Christian said sarcastically.

Carl laughed a little with him and walked closer to the cell. "Now, Hope, you are trying to be hurtful. Why don't you let the soldier go?"

Christian tightened the hold he had on the soldier's neck. "I think I am just going to have to snap his neck." The soldier started to panic as he tried to get out of Christian's hold, but Christian was too powerful.

Carl chuckled and stared at him. "Go ahead. I want to see you do that."

Christian just stayed there, holding the soldier.

Carl looked at him as if he was looking right into his soul. "I do not think you have the nerve. You kill him, and I will have this guard here shoot an arrow at Ben and kill him. It doesn't matter to me, so you decide what you are going to do."

Christian released his grip and let the soldier go.

Carl smiled. "I knew you were not going to hurt that soldier. It is not your style. Don't try to be something you are not. Now help the soldier put on your leg shackles. You have an important engagement to attend for all the people to see."

Christian did not fight the soldier while the shackles were being applied. Once this was done, another soldier opened the cell door, and they dragged Hope out of the cell.

Carl said, "You should have seen your face when you did not find any type of weapon on these guards. I'm still laughing inside thinking about it. Do you think I would have given you a chance like that? Now let's go to the courtyard for your special performance. Please don't fight on the way. That would be below you, and I would rather ... well, if you want to get beaten more than once, then act up. I am sure the soldier you beat would like to hurt you. Right now would be a good time since you're in restraints. So act up or make your way to the courtyard peacefully."

Christian did not fight with the guards as they went straight to the courtyard. When Christian walked out, people stared with worry, and women started to weep. They knew Christian was the one who had changed things around and made their lives better. Now they were worried for him and worried about what was to come.

Soldiers were everywhere; they encircled the townspeople in the courtyard. The townspeople's faces dropped, and people became quiet as they saw Christian being brought to the center of the plaza in shackles and chains. The soldiers secured Christian's arms in the pillory, and they got ready to whip him. Just then, a man ran toward Hope in an attempt to free him, but before the man could get close, he was struck down by an arrow. The man fell to the ground hard, his life ended. No one ran to him; fear had taken over. A soldier started to whip Hope. The townspeople became horrified as they watched the whip rip into Hope's skin. Two other men ran to help him, but they were struck down by arrows as well.

Brutus stood on a balcony that overlooked the courtyard. He walked forward and spoke to the crowd, "Now, my townspeople, let's not be rash. Do run to your death. You now have a new ruler, and it is I. The life you have under my rule will be about the same as the life you had with King William. The only difference will be that you will give proper respect to my soldiers. Now, Hope, why not tell these people not to interfere while you are being punished? I sure would hate for another one of them to die because of you."

Carl, the soldier who had been whipping Christian, held back for a moment as Christian pleaded, "Do not interfere with my fate. Do not sacrifice your lives for mine."

Carl resumed whipping Hope, each lash ripping Hope's flesh apart. Blood dripped from the old and new wounds. The whip just continued to tear his back apart. Hope kept on fighting the pain and would not scream. Blood ran down his back and dripped on the ground. The townspeople mourned and cried because their savior from King William was being badly beaten. After a while, Hope was having a hard time holding himself up. Carl saw this and stopped whipping and looked at Brutus. Carl knew Christian was not going to ask for mercy or show any weakness. Christian would fight as much as he could. "Take him back to the dungeon," said Brutus. He turned to the people. "Now, townspeople, I hope you will respect your new ruler. The more obedient you are, the safer your Hope will be." Brutus stared down at the crowd.

Hope did not shed any tears or cry out loud. The people stood still and were speechless for they did not want to anger anyone. They were obedient. The soldiers helped Christian out of the pillory and walked him back to the dungeon. Once in the dungeon, the soldiers opened the cell door. "Ben, here is your cellmate," said one of the soldiers. "Take care of him for it seems he will be needed again later." They dropped him on the floor and took off his shackles and other restraints.

Ben saw Christian's wounds and said to the retreating soldiers, "What did you do to him?" When they did not answer, he murmured, "Help me, God." Ben's face was filled with worry, and he started to take care of the wounds. Christian was in severe pain but did not show it in any way. He did not want his captives to feel satisfaction from what they had done. With a calm voice, Ben said, "Don't worry. I will take care of you." Hope fell asleep while Ben dressed his wounds.

THE BIRTH

"Go get Florence. It is time for me to have the baby, Samuel." Mary lay in her bed waiting to give birth to her first child.

"Yes, my dear." Samuel ran out of their hut. Ten minutes later, Samuel returned with the midwife. Florence could see the pain in Mary's eyes; she knew the woman was ready to give birth to her baby. In a calm and comforting voice, she asked, "How are you doing?"

"The baby is ready to come, and my water just broke." Mary moaned in pain. "I need to push."

Florence got into position, "You will be able to do this. Do not worry. I have delivered quite a few babies. Now let's deliver this baby." Mary listened and started to push. Through all her pain, her baby appeared. Florence smiled. "You are doing great. Look—it's a boy!"

"Let me have him," Mary cried in excitement. She turned to her husband. "Samuel, here is our son."

"He looks great. I am so proud of you, Mary." Samuel walked toward them and embraced them. Mary noticed a birthmark on the inside of the baby's right wrist. "Samuel, look at this birthmark." Samuel looked closer at the baby's right wrist and saw the birthmark. Florence started to shake a little because she knew of the monk's dream. This dream had been told to King William, and he knew who the midwives were. Florence began to get ready to leave.

Samuel noticed how Florence was acting and stood up. "Wait! Why are you leaving so fast?"

Florence tried to hide her nervousness. "I have somewhere else to go."

Samuel shook his head no and replied, "No you don't. Are you ready to send a newborn baby to its death. It is just a birthmark. I don't care if there was mention of a child with a birthmark who will save its people. How many years ago was that? Are you going to tell the soldiers?" Samuel walked closer to Florence. "I know you know who I was once and that a child with a birthmark came to be mine. Still, it is a child of God as you are. Are you so ready to have that life taken away?"

Florence sulked. Mary saw what was going on and looked at Florence with wet, worried eyes. Florence saw this and started to melt, for in her heart, she could not let an innocent child be murdered. Mary noticed Florence's demeanor change, so she asked, "What do you want to name the baby, Samuel?"

Samuel picked up his son and held him high in the air above his head. He smiled at his newborn baby. "We will call him Christian."

Florence shook her head. "After a religion. You sure are looking for trouble. Maybe even death."

Samuel lowered his son and gave him back to Mary. In a tone full of peace, he said, "I know what was said about the birthmark. It was not determined where on the body it was located. If there is any truth in the prophesy, my son will be ready. He will learn about the Christian religion even though Christian teachings are not now tolerated and there are no churches. All I ask is that you do not tell anyone for my family's sake. If you do, you will be responsible for what happens to us. We will keep his wrists covered up so the birthmark cannot be seen."

Florence calmed herself down a little, but she was still nervous. As she looked at the child, a feeling of peace and love came to her as it did every time she delivered a newborn. "I will not say anything." Florence then left the hut.

Mary looked at her husband with soft eyes. "Are you sure that is wise, Samuel, to call our son Christian?"

"My dear," Samuel responded as he looked right at Mary, "our child is in God's hands. In the past, I ran and hid to keep from being killed instead of dying for what I believe. I will not make that mistake again. I want to make my Holy Father proud of me." Samuel humbled himself even more. "I was a monk. I know the Bible inside and out. I haven't felt as close to God as I do now in such a long time. I love God with all my heart, and if our child is to be the one, I will do what I must even if it means sacrificing my life."

Mary sighed. "All right, Samuel, we will call him Christian."

Samuel hugged his wife and picked up his newborn son. "God, this is your son. I dedicate him to you. Help me take care of him." Samuel then lowered Christian into Mary's arms.

Mary smiled and touched Samuel's arm. "Everything will be fine. We will have a good son devoted to God. We will keep his birthmark covered." Mary thought for a little. "When he gets bigger, I will sew two wristbands for him to wear. One will say 'God Loves You' and on the other 'Love God.' I will make them big so I can adjust them as he grows. He will wear them when he is outside, and I will clean them at night. If they wear out, I will make new ones. You see, Samuel, I love God too, and I believe you." There were soft tears in her eyes. Samuel again held his family in his arms as tears fell down his face.

***

Years passed, and Christian was raised in a loving family. He followed his father's footsteps and learned to be a farmer. Samuel taught him about the Bible. He taught Christian to speak and write Latin and English. Christian was truly happy. Even if they lived in a hut and did not have much, he felt the warmth of his family. Soldiers came to their home and took whatever they wanted from them, leaving just enough food so they could keep working and providing food for the soldiers. Christian one day asked, "Dad, why do they take our food and property? Why don't they respect other people's property? Is not one of God's commandments—You shall not steal."

Samuel looked at Christian "You are right, my son, but not everyone follows God's commandments. We are living in a kingdom where might makes right. Our king took away our religion, and he now controls us with fear. That is why you see the soldiers coming here as often as they do."

Christian thought for a little. "Dad, what can be done with men like that in charge?"

Samuel smiled at his son. "Pray for them. Have faith in God for God can perform miracles and change people's hearts. Now let's pray, son." They both got on their knees, closed their eyes, and put their hands together. Samuel prayed aloud: "Our Father in heaven, hallowed be your name, your kingdom come, your will be done, on earth as it is in heaven. Give us today our daily bread. Forgive us our debts, as we also have forgiven our debtors. And lead us not into temptation, but deliver us from evil one. God, I ask you to help our king and keep him healthy. I ask you that he sees his people and wants to do better for them. I thank you for providing for us. In Jesus's name I pray. Amen."

"Dad, why you pray for the king?" Christian looked at him in confusion. "Is he not the one causing all this hardship?"

Samuel looked at his son and softly replied, "The king is just a man. He is not perfect. None of us is. In time, I hope he sees the error of his ways. Things can happen to people to change their hearts for good or bad. I am asking for a miracle, and God can provide."

"Why do you not wish bad things for him father?" Christian asked.

Samuel frowned. "Son, what good would it do to wish harm on others? You must not wrong those who wrong you, or those you suspect will wrong you. We our all God's children. We are all sinners, and we all must repent." Samuel placed his hand on his son's head and rubbed his hair. "You are a good son—a son any father would be proud of. Remember that, son. Let's go to bed."

One day, Samuel and Christian were working in the fields when they saw Benjamin, one of their neighbors in the road with his cart and donkey. Suddenly, one of the wheels came off. Samuel walked to him and said, "Do you need some help, Benjamin?"

Benjamin smiled for he was happy to see his friend come to his aid. "Yes, I do." Samuel and Christian lifted the cart a bit so Benjamin could put the wheel back on. As Christian set the cart back down, the edge of the cart floor caught on his right wristband, and Benjamin saw the birthmark on his wrist. Benjamin giggled a little. "What is so funny, Benjamin?" Samuel asked.

Benjamin acted as if he was in a hurry. "Nothing is wrong. Thanks for your help. I must carry on with my tasks." Benjamin left whistling joyfully as if something had greatly cheered him up. Samuel and Christian watched him for a little and then went back to work in the field.

Later that night, Benjamin stopped at the tavern. After a few drinks, he started to feel pretty good, and he began to boast, "I saw a boy with a birthmark on his right wrist." He danced around a little, feeling pretty good. "I saw the one that will take down the king! He is living among us," Benjamin said loudly. One of the other patrons left the tavern to tell the king's soldiers.

The king's men arrived at the tavern and walked right up to Benjamin. A soldier put his arm on Ben's shoulder and said, "Come with us." It was an order Benjamin could not refuse. His face changed colors, there was fear in his eyes, and he almost lost the strength in his knees. One of the soldiers took the drink from Ben's hand and put it on the bar. The soldiers escorted Benjamin outside. Outside, one of the soldiers stared him straight in his eyes, and said, "I hear you were telling people you saw the one will take down the king. I hear you were boastful about it." Benjamin started to shake nervously. "Did you not say this? Answer now if you don't want to lose a limb!"

Benjamin knew he was caught; he let his fear control him. He could not do anything, so he answered, "Yes."

"Where is he then?" asked the soldier. Benjamin did not reply; he did not want to be responsible for anything bad that might happen to the child and his family. The soldiers asked again, but Benjamin still refused to tell them. The soldiers started to push him and put fear in him. "Don't want to tell us?" asked one soldier. He turned to the other soldier. "Take him over to the horse trough." The soldier pushed Benjamin until he got to the horse trough. Then he dumped Benjamin into it. "Let's see if a little water will help your memory." The soldier held Benjamin's head under the water and then pulled it up. "Are you not going to answer me? I can do this for a long time." The soldier chuckled. Benjamin struggled, but the soldier was too powerful. The other soldier said, "Hold his head under water. Let's see how long he can hold his breath." The soldier pushed him under the water, and Benjamin really struggled. He was soon not fighting back as much, so the soldier pulled his head out of the water. Benjamin started to cough and spit out water from his mouth. "Are you ready to answer our questions now?" The soldier pulled Benjamin's face closer to him. Benjamin was panting; he had no more fight in him. He could not control his fear. "Now show us where this boy lives—this boy you claim has the mark on his wrist."

Benjamin nodded his head. They got into a cart and rode out to Samuel's farm. Benjamin raised his hand reluctantly, pointed with fear, and slumped down on the seat. "There it is. Now will you let me go?" Benjamin spoke in a sad voice.

The soldiers looked at him. One of them smiled. "No, we cannot do that. You are going to the dungeon. If I were you, I might not want to leave. I am sure the king has something special planned for you. Thanks to you, we now know who this prophesy is about." They went on their way to the dungeon. Benjamin became lifeless because his drinking and boasting had caused so much damage. "You know the king does not like loose ends. He will deal with that family," said the soldier. At the dungeon, they had to carry him down the stone steps because he could barely move. One soldier said to the dungeon guard, "Here is a weak and pitiful man who turned in a kid to save his own skin. I'm sure you know what we're going to do to him and his family. Take him away. I am done with him." Benjamin's head sunk to his chest in disappointment. He did not put up any fight. He just entered the cell and started to cry.

The next day, Brutus and the king showed up with the soldiers outside the hut on Samuel's farm. One soldier said, "In there, my king, is a child with a birthmark on his right wrist."

The king looked at the soldier. "What do you know of this family?"

The soldier answered, "They never give us grief over whatever we take. From what I hear, Samuel is a religious man. He could be one of those monks who escaped when King Archibald had all the monks at the monastery killed."

The king responded, "A religious man. Have you told anyone of this?"

Both soldiers replied, "No."

The king put his head up high and said, "Good. Keep it that way. As for the one who told you, he can remain in the dungeon for now."

One of the soldiers looked at the king and asked, "What are you going to do?"

The king looked at him with a stern expression. "Are you questioning me?"

"No, my king." The soldier cowered because he knew he had been out of line. The king looked at Brutus, and they moved away from the soldiers.

Brutus looked at the king. "What is your plan? Do you want to leave things as they are and take a chance?" Brutus already knew what the king's answer was going to be. The king did not like to have any loose ends and would not risk losing his kingship—especially from a little child. The king informed the two soldiers of his plan. They were not happy about it, but they knew it would cost them their lives if they did not follow orders.

Upon orders from the king, the two soldiers left the area and came back as one of the townspeople. They stormed into the hut with swords in their hands. One man went straight to Samuel. Samuel grabbed a chair and started to defend himself. He knocked over a candle, and a fire started in the hut. He was unable to get to his wife or child. The other soldier went right to Mary and cut her down. She fell to the floor, looking directly at Christian. She died immediately.

Samuel yelled, "No!" The fire started to grow. Samuel looked at Christian. "Run, my son." Together, the two soldiers killed Samuel. Then they turned to look for Christian. Christian had already jumped out a window and run to the people he saw outside. He saw two men on horseback in the distance, but others had been attracted to the area because of the fire. The king and Brutus saw this. Two men started running after Christian with their swords in their hands. The king and Brutus, who were both on horseback, took out their bows and shot the men. Both fell, but one of the men tried to speak. The king shot another arrow at the man. The arrow pierced the man's heart, killing him instantly.

The king got off his horse and said, "You are safe now, my son."

Christian was weeping uncontrollably and embraced the king, "My parents are in there." The hut was engulfed in fire.

The king put his arm around Christian's shoulders and said, "I will take care of you." Christian continued to sob for he knew his parents were both dead, and nothing would bring them back.

Brutus picked up the two dead men and threw them onto his horse. He led his horse close to the burning hut and threw the bodies into the fire. The king nodded at Brutus, but one loose end remained, and that was Christian. The king knew that, if he killed Christian now, the people would retaliate. He knew that, if Christian were to die soon, his death could also be the end of his reign. So, the king held Christian close, more to put on a show than to provide comfort. Christian looked at the king and said through his sobs, "Thanks for saving me, but my parents are dead. I have nowhere to go."

The king looked at him. "I will take care of you." Christian hugged the king again. The king felt different after everything that had happened, and he felt some regret for what he had done. He never let anyone close to him; he remained always guarded. He knew only about war.

Over the next few years, Christian changed the kingdom with the love he had in his heart. He changed the king's heart and encouraged him to be kind to his people and not to harm them. Brutus and his loyal soldiers did not like this. They were used to taking whatever they wanted, but the king stopped them from continuing this practice. During this time, the king shared with Christian all of knowledge he had of the kingdom and its territory.

Over the passing years, Brutus wanted more. Inside, he had always wanted to be king. He had liked the way it had been before when citizens cowered in his presence because they were afraid. "Is this the direction you decided to take?" he asked the king one day. "I thought the plan was to keep everything as it was."

"Time has changed me," answered the king.

"You had his parents murdered, killed the soldiers that did it, and then took the son of the parents you murdered as your own. A boy you had considered killing. Now is that some sick shit? Maybe someone should let Christian know what really happened," Brutus threatened.

The king stood boldly and looked down at Brutus. "Do not repeat what you just said. If you do, those will be the last words you speak."

Brutus eyes opened wide, and he became defensive. "After all the years I have been loyal to you, this is how you talk to me? Remember that I was the one who helped you with the plan to deal with Christian. If something happens to me, that information will be leaked."

The king stepped closer to Brutus and put one hand on his sword. "Do not try to intimidate me."

Brutus left the room abruptly. From then on, Brutus always

made sure he had a few of his loyal soldiers with him wherever he went.

One day, the king was walking down the stairs to the beach with Christian. They encountered a soldier on his way up from the beach. They all stood still. The king had been talking with Christian and was absorbed in their conversation. Suddenly, the soldier drew his sword and started to attack the king. He addressed the king: "Look at my face. Do I not look familiar?"

The king's face flushed because he knew it was the brother of the soldier who had been murdered a few years ago when Christian's parents had been killed. The king was able to move away from the attack, but he fell down a few steps. The soldier followed him.

"Any last words for my brother, king?" The soldier walked down the steps with his back toward Christian. He was about to fatally strike the prone monarch. The soldier was so focused on hate and killing the king that he did not pay attention to Christian. Christian carried a small sword that he used to play soldier with. He drew the sword and pushed the point into the soldier's back. The soldier arched his back in agony and dropped his sword. The king quickly grabbed the sword, jumped up, and struck down the man before he could speak.

"My boy," said the king. "I love you, son." The king gave Christian a big hug. "You saved my life!" Christian was overwhelmed with happiness because he had been able to save someone he loved. He had prevented someone he cared for from being murdered and taken away from him for good.

Soon the king acquired thirteen brand new soldiers who were loyal only to Christian and him alone. One day, the king went to Christian and said, "I want you to learn how to fight. You are thirteen now. I'm going to send you away from here to a place where you will be safe. There you will meet the finest swordsmen, and they will teach you.

A sadness and sense of abandonment consumed Christian. "I do not want to leave you."

The king looked at him. "You will be fine, and so will I. I want you to be stronger than I am. I will feel safer with you away from here until I get things figured out."

"All right, Father," Christian said sadly as he dropped his head.

The king lifted his head up lovingly. "It will be for only a little while."

The next day, Christian was placed on a boat that immediately set sail for the city of Svantovit.

CHRISTIAN
RETURNS

After seven years passed, Christian finally returned to his homeland. He was no longer the small kid he'd been when he left. He was now twenty years old, six foot one, and built like a Greek god. He had muscle on top of muscle, but he was still agile and fast. He had gained endurance and could run forever. His face was chiseled like a sculpture. He had short brown hair and brown eyes. As for his swordsmanship, there was no one who could beat him. He had many years ahead of him, and he used his sword to stay alive. He'd had a darkness in him before he left Kyrre, but he had been made whole because of an innocent.

Christian already had a nickname, but he did not want anyone to know it. The nickname did not bring hope to anyone; rather, it brought fear. Good people in Svantovit who had known him for the past few years felt he was bloodthirsty and loved taking people's lives. Others honored him as a god because of what he could achieve with the sword. This was not what Christian had wanted. The happiest times in his life had been when he was on his farm with his family. They had not had much luxury, but they had shared great love.

When the boat carrying Christian came in sight of his homeland, a smile came back to his face that had not been seen for quite some time. He looked at the beach and the cliffs with the stairs going to the castle. In the spring air, he could smell the flowers that grew naturally. The boat reached the harbor and rested next to the dock, rocking a little from the waves until it was tied up. Once the plank was put down, Christian ran onto the land. He could see King William and ran toward him. King William went to him with open arms. "I am so happy to see you, my son. Boy, you sure have grown! I am now looking up to you!" They embraced each other.

"Dad, I am happy to see you too. It has been a long time," Christian said happily. "I have missed you so much and this place as well. I did not like the pace of things in the big city." The king and Christian started to walk toward the castle. Christian felt an immense weight being lifted from his shoulders now that he was back at home. He felt he was out of the reach of King Archibald.

King William looked at Christian. "I have a place set up for you, and the people are happy about your arrival." The king then stopped walking. "Listen, I know some of the things you did in Svantovit over these past years. King Archibald made sure he told me. He wanted to rub it in my face that I had sent you there, and he boasted about what you did for him. We do not need to discuss it. Only if you want to. I know you are not that way. I am glad to see the happiness in your face as it was the day before I told you I was sending you away."

Christian was hesitant to say anything. He was just so happy about being home. He knew people were not perfect and remembered the king had told him he had been sent away to keep him safe. He did think about it and felt that, if King William had known the outcome, he would not have sent him. So, he humbled himself and did not say a word about it.

King William looked at him with sadness. Others would have complained about what they had gone through in life. "Christian, I am sorry I failed you in the end. I did not know that was going to happen, and I was not powerful enough to challenge King Archibald and get you back any sooner. I did ask about your return, but he ignored my requests."

Christian looked at King William. "Dad, it's okay. I am as strong as you wanted me to be, and I know how to use this sword. I took advantage of the opportunity that was given to me, and I studied books as well as swordsmanship. I learned about warfare and different languages." Christian paused, and he felt darkness come on him. "I learned a lot about combat from books and from practicing it. I did not want to stop. My anger drove me to become something I did not like. I liked the power I had when I succumbed to destruction. I forgot about what my father Samuel taught me. The bad thing is that King Archibald noticed. He took advantage of it."

King William replied, "Son, you are now home. Let us put that behind us."

The next day, Christian was walking in the courtyard when he saw some of King William's personal soldiers. They were practicing with swords. They were Curtis, Joseph, Cassian, Crispin, Alexander, and Bard. Curtis called for Christian to join them; he was their leader. He was six foot four inches tall and did not fear anyone. He used his brawn to his advantage, but still he was quick for his large size. He rushed into any situation because he feared nothing and relied on his size to take care of things.

Curtis again called Christian to join them. Christian went to them reluctantly. Curtis said, "Look at the pup! He is all grown up. Looks like he has a little muscle on him."

Christian smiled and replied, "You still have the same big mouth. I'm surprised you haven't lost any teeth yet." The other soldiers started laughing.

Joseph was laughing the hardest and jumped into the conversation. "It seems he has you figured out, Curtis." Joseph was the second in command. He was not as big as Curtis, but he was still six feet tall. He was good at planning things, and he was proficient with both sword and bow.

Curtis smirked and felt he needed to embarrass Christian. "I see you have a few swords on you. Do you know how to use them or are they just for decoration?"

Christian looked at him and thought to himself, *Curtis is going to challenge me.* "I know how to use them very well."

Curtis waved him over to where he was. "Let us see, pup."

Christian shook his head and laughed. "After we are done, you are going to have to figure out a different name for me. Pup is not going to work."

Christian drew his long sword from the scabbard and started to spar with Curtis. Curtis swung at Christian, barely missing him. Christian fell back, stumbling a little. Curtis started to smile because he felt he had an advantage over Christian. Christian was running from him. Curtis started to get overconfident. "Is that all you have?" Curtis swung his sword at Christian again. All of a sudden, Christian smacked Curtis's sword out of his hand and pointed his sword at Curtis's neck. Curtis laughed. "You were playing with me all this time, letting me think I could win."

Christian lowered his sword from Curtis's neck. "I used your cockiness to win against you. It was simple. You were a little too confident in yourself, especially when you were facing an opponent you had never spared with before."

Curtis shook himself. "Let us try one more time."

Christian accepted the challenge. This time, Christian did not play around with Curtis. He had Curtis on the run and counted the moves that he could have killed him with.

Curtis, realizing he was no match for Christian, wanted to see what the boy could do against two opponents. "Can I have Joseph also spar with me against you?"

Christian agreed. He put his long sword back in his scabbard and grabbed the two long knives he carried on his back. One was the first weapon he made that was the size of a sword. He liked using them when fighting more than two people because they were equally balanced, and he was able to strike with both arms. All of his swords felt like extensions of his arms. Christian started to move the knives around. "Let's start."

Curtis and Joseph both came at Christian. Christian stopped

both of their strikes and was able to guide Joseph's sword toward Curtis. Curtis moved backward quickly to avoid the blade. Christian, now behind Joseph, knocked him down. Christian told Joseph he was dead. Christian then went for Curtis. Curtis could see the hunger in Christian's eyes, and he stopped. "Well, I can see when I am bested."

Christian stood a little taller. "So, what are you going to call me now that pup doesn't fit?"

Curtis laughed. "You are still a pup. Maybe a pup that can beat me, but still a pup."

Joseph got up. His face had gone cold. "So it is true of what has been said."

Curtis looked at Joseph in discontent. "Be quiet, Joseph. Christian, you are with family now."

Christian smiled. "Thanks. You do not know how good it is to be home." He sighed. "I want to put that whole other life behind me."

Curtis became more serious. "What are your plans now?"

Christian replied, "To help our people. I have seen too much in my time. I know I am young. My years away were not all good. I know you have heard about me. I hate to say it is true. I have killed many in the arena and was King Archibald's assassin. I need to know I can change that. I need to feel good about myself again."

Curtis looked at his crew. "We will not bring up your past. You are at home now."

Christian walked away. Once he was out of sight, Curtis said to Joseph, "Our boy is a killer now. I did not have a chance to attack him."

Joseph replied, "Well he knocked me down and pretended to kill me. I have not seen anyone move like that."

"Let's not tell anyone about this. I feel Christian is going to have to be a killer again soon. Something is unfolding."

***

A month passed, and Christian started to feel at more ease. He slowed down on his training. He started to feel he did not need to use his sword. One day, Brutus went to the king and told him about a new town setting up a half day's ride away. Some of the villagers were moving there. Brutus persuaded the king that he needed to take action to stop this. If he did not, there would be no one to take care of the needs of Kyrre.

The king approached Christian, "I need you to go with Brutus to see what is going on. If the people in the new town are a threat, they must be destroyed."

Christian was not happy about this. "From what I heard, it is just a small village. How can they be a threat?"

The king replied, "Just go check it out." Christian left with a contingent of king's men.

THE TRUTH
COMES OUT

A day later, the king's men approached the new village at sunup. The villagers were just waking up and starting their morning. The group slowly entered the village. Some villagers ran for the woods. One of them approached Brutus and said, "How can we help you? I see the numbers you have, and we are no match for you. Neither are we a threat." The man started to get nervous for he saw the uneasiness in Carl's eyes. He spoke again. "I see you are from Kyrre. Can we help you, my lord?"

Brutus felt power. He missed people acting cowardly. "I want you to leave this place at once or you will be destroyed." The man began to question Brutus, but Brutus immediately knocked the guy down to the ground with his sword. Other soldiers got off their horses and started to attack the villagers.

Christian got off his horse. He tried to stop soldiers from killing by yelling, "What are you doing? These people are not of any concern to us. They have no army. There is no glory or honor in killing these people!"

Brutus started to get angry with Christian. "They will become a threat if not put in their place now."

Christian glared at Brutus. "What are they going to do? Throw sticks and stones at the castle walls? I do not see anything that could breach the walls or help them succeed in an attack on our soldiers."

Brutus sighed with discontent. He turned to the bugler. "Blow the horn to call the soldiers back." The young man blew on his bugle the signal to summon them back. Brutus looked at one of the main buildings. "It looks like Carl is having too much fun and is not stopping."

Christian saw this also. "I will go get him."

Brutus replied, "Carl might like that." Christian took off after Carl with Thomas. Thomas was five years older than Christian. Thomas's parents were carpenters but also liked to work in the fields. At times in the past, they would come over to Samuel's farm and visit. Thomas himself was a carpenter by heart but had a desire to try and be a soldier. So, Christian had trained him, and they had spared together.

Carl entered the main lodge and started to look around. He heard someone in there. He looked around and moved a few pieces of furniture. "Come out if you dare. I will find you if you do not. I do like the hunt." Carl then heard a sound coming from under a wooden bench. He threw the bench aside and found a boy who appeared to be about twelve years old lying on the ground. Carl grimaced. "Stand up, boy." Carl was hoping for a challenge, and all he got was this little boy. The boy stood up. Shaking, he looked at Carl. He did not say anything. Carl stared into his eyes. "Do you want to beg for your life?" The boy did not reply; he just stood there. Carl became amused. "This is going to be fun." Carl lifted his sword and made a bloody mark on the boy's face.

Right then, Christian stormed into the lodge with Thomas, surprising Carl. "You finally found someone you can defeat. Wait— he might be too much of a challenge for you."

Carl got angry. "Leave if you know what's good for you."

"Now, Carl, do not be so rude. Let us have some fun ourselves," replied Christian.

Carl was still focused on harming the child. "If you do not leave, I will finish you after I finish him, little prince."

Christian walked closer to him. "You put one more mark on that boy, and you will not see tomorrow. So, finish me first, and then you can have your fun."

Carl turned and approached Christian. They started to raise their swords and began to circle each other. Every move Carl made, Christian blocked, and he called off strikes he made that could kill Carl. Carl realized he did not have a chance with Christian. Christian slapped Carl on his hand with the side of his sword, causing Carl to drop his sword. Carl was then standing over his sword, and Christian was within striking range. Christian sternly said, "If you go for your sword, I will kill you. Now I should finish you as you thought you were going to finish me. Let me think this one through. Just stand there being unsure. If you aren't scared, you should be. How does it feel when someone is standing over you with a sword and you are defenseless?" Carl did not reply but was shaking hard. "I know what I will do now," Christian replied. Christian took his sword and cut Carl across his face as he had cut the boy. Christian replied, "Now leave without your sword. It will be returned to you later. I will not tell anyone about this incident. You can tell them one of the people you cut down left you that injury."

Carl stormed out of the lodge covering his face. When he got to his horse, Brutus saw the bleeding cut. "What happened to your face?"

Carl replied, "One of the townspeople was hiding behind the door and got a swipe at me before I took him down."

Brutus did not believe him. "Right. All right, soldiers, let's head back to the castle."

Once Carl left, Thomas said, "Come here, boy, and I will take care of your wound. It's all right. I have a son close to your age. He is as spirited as you are. You were very strong to stand up to that soldier and not show any weakness. I will not hurt you." The boy approached Thomas and let him start to clean his cut. "What is your name?" Thomas asked.

"My name is Robert. Do you know if my father is dead?" he asked nervously because he was afraid of the answer.

"We do not know. Let me first take care of your cut, and we will look for him." Thomas tended to the boy's wound. As the soldiers were leaving, a hunter ran toward the lodge. Thomas glanced at the boy and then looked at Christian. "I think I am a going stop being a soldier and take up being a carpenter."

"Why?" asked Christian.

Thomas looked harder at Robert. "Because of my son. My wife is passing, and I need to be there to take care of him."

"You will have to turn in your sword. If things ever change in our kingdom, soldiers will bother you, especially since you were loyal to me." The thing Christian feared most was being defenseless.

"I know, but my son needs me." Thomas was convincing himself thoroughly as he took care of Robert.

The hunter entered the lodge and started to walk toward them with vengeance on his face. Robert noticed him. "Stop, Father! I am fine. These soldiers saved my life and are taking care of me."

"What happened to this town?" the hunter asked in a demanding tone.

As Christian was about to reply, Robert interrupted him. "Dad, you should have seen the sword fight that happened here. I have never seen anyone handle a sword the way he did!" The hunter looked at Christian and asked him, "Have you been at Svantovit?"

"I have been there." Christian's eyes opened wider.

"I have seen you at your best. I know who you are. So, are you doing the same at King William's request?" The hunter asked bluntly.

Christian stood up and got ready. "This was the work of King William's second in command, Brutus. He persuaded the king to do this because of a fake threat they made up."

"Dad, this man stopped them and saved my life," Robert replied frantically.

"Who cut my son?" the hunter asked. He was obviously becoming more enraged as he moved closer to Christian.

"His name is Carl," replied Christian.

"Dad, you must listen to me! This man was willing to fight to the death for me. The soldier that did this has a fresh cut on his face just as big as mine. Please, Dad, calm down. I am begging you," cried out Robert trying to get his dad to listen.

The hunter eased off as he thought about everything that had been said, "My name is Edmund. Thanks for saving my son's life. Robert, come here and let me see you." Robert went to his dad and gave him a hug. "Let me look you over, Robert." Edmund looked his son over and said, "You will be fine. Might have a scar, but that is all."

Christian eased up a little and said, "I am sorry this happened. If you are willing to listen to me, I can tell you of a place that not many know about. It is an old castle ruins about three days' ride east of here. If you could go straight northeast from the castle it would be a day's ride, but the cliffs prevent that route. You must go to the mountain passage and just head east. I have seen the place. King William took me there once so I would know about. It in case anything bad happened, I would know where to go."

"I will gather my remaining people and take them there. It will take us a while to get ready." Edmund sighed. "I do believe you because I know that, if you wanted us all dead, I would not be standing here in front of you right now. We met before at the arena, but I changed my mind after seeing you." Edmund took another breath because he had almost let his anger take him away from the one thing he loved the most, his son. "Let's leave this lodge but let me go out first just in case any of my people are out there waiting," Edmund led the way out. Christian and Thomas followed, got on their horses, and left for the castle. Edmund went looking for the rest of his people. Edmund was able to gather them and persuade them to go with him to the castle ruins.

The next day, Christian and Thomas arrived back at the castle. Thomas resigned his position as soldier and went to be with his family. Christian entered the castle and saw the king, who said, "I heard from Brutus already that they were no threat now and will not turn into a threat."

"It was a massacre. No one was fighting back. All they did was run away or be killed. There was no honor in what was done," claimed Christian.

The king sighed and did not show any empathy. "They now will never be a concern."

Christian's face changed in disbelief. "This is not the father that I left years ago. This is not what I want to be. What was done was the way I handled things for King Archibald. I do not want to go back to that life." Christian turned around and walked away hastily. The king started to sadden for upsetting Christian and called for him, but Christian kept walking.

A few days later, Brutus ran into Christian. "I heard you talked to the king. He told me you did not like what was done in the new village. You did not like the way the king took the news. This is the way the king has always been. I should say this is the way the king was before he knew you. You should ask the king about how your family died."

Christian's entire demeanor started to change. "I am sure you were not involved at all. This must be a plan to get me to do something. I am sure if the king was involved, you probably told him."

Brutus put up his hands. "You might not want to start something until you have all the facts. Go talk to King William and see what he has to say." Christian headed toward the castle to see the king.

On his way to the castle, Christian ran into Curtis. Curtis noticed the rage in Christian's eyes. He said, "What is it?"

Christian cut him off frantically, "Find your men and leave now. Do not delay. Do not think you need to guard the king. A takeover is imminent, and you do not have enough people to save anyone. Curtis, take your men and ride for a half day north to a village that was destroyed by Brutus. If you do not see anyone, head east for three days. If you see soldiers behind you, they were not sent by me.

They were sent to kill all of you. Continue riding north till either you lose them or kill them. The directions I have given you are to an old castle ruin. The villagers that were attacked could be living there. The leader's name is Edmund. Tell him my name and that you come in peace."

"What are you talking about?" Curtis took a stance. "My duty is to keep the king safe."

Christian's face became more serious, and he looked at Curtis with piercing eyes. "The king ordered the murder of my family years ago. And he ordered the murder of the villagers at the new village that was destroyed a few days ago. Brutus I am sure was involved in all of it. Curtis, our people and I need you to live to help us. If you do not leave right away, Brutus will have you killed. He is waiting till I confront the king. Go now!"

Curtis looked at him and left. He soon gathered his men and departed. Once they were gone, Christian went to speak with the king.

Christian entered the king's chambers. Without any hesitation, and with seriousness in his voice, he said, "Brutus and I had an interesting conversation just a moment ago. I know his purpose for it. He wants to take over this kingdom."

King William looked at him. "Problem is, there are men who are now loyal to him who were once loyal to me."

Christian looked right at him. "I do not really want to stop him. He told me who commanded my parents' deaths." The king started to turn white for he had always feared this day would come. Christian held up his right wrist and pulled at his wristband. "All because of a certain mark I have on my wrist and the myth of the monk's dream about it." As Christian started to get more and more worked up, he started to walk toward the king. The king stepped backwards. Christian went on to say, "You are the one who created me. You made me a killer. I have killed so many men. I took out a few nobles so that their people would bow down to King Archibald." Christian walked even closer to the king. "You could have left me as

I was with my family. I would have remained a simple farmer who would not have been any threat to you. My father always prayed for you. He did not wish you to be harmed; rather, he prayed that you would change." Christian's hand went to the grip of his sword. In rage, he said, "I became what you feared! Well, King William, you might as well finish the job and kill me."

The king was still walking backward and was dangerously close to the edge of the balcony. Christian took his hand off his sword grip, stopped moving forward, and shook his head. He lowered his voice in disgust. "To think I told you I loved you. I saved your life! I loved you and saved the life of the one who killed my mother and father. How sick is that?" The king did not say a word. Guilt finally filled his heart, for he truly had come to love Christian. He had never been loved before. Because of his emotions, he was not aware of where he was standing, and he suddenly slipped and fell over the balcony. Christian ran to grab him, but he was too late. A few soldiers had seen the king fall, and they saw Christian on the balcony. "It was Christian!" one of them cried out. Soldiers went to seize Christian. He did not put up a fight and was taken to the dungeon. Brutus was soon informed of what had happened. Brutus smiled. His time had come.

SURVIVAL: FIGHT
OR FLIGHT

"Ben, how is our Hope doing?" Brutus asked.

"He is still alive, but you hurt him badly."

"It appears it was just enough. He is still living." Brutus oozed sarcasm. He turned to a guard. "Soldier, let me know when he awakens. I need to talk to him." Brutus departed while Ben continued to look after Christian.

***

"Curtis, are they still on our trail?" Joseph asked as they rode north.

"It appears that way. There are about twenty-four soldiers riding after us. I do not think it is any type of greeting party. I am sure something happened to Christian. He saved us. Let's keep riding north. We'll have to find a place to fight or lose them." Curtis raised his arm and motioned for his men to keep on going.

***

The next morning, Christian woke up disoriented. He could barely move. "You need to eat, Hope. You need to keep up your strength. Here have some of this food," said Ben. Christian ate the food slowly and drank some water. "That is good, Hope. Keep it up. You will get better."

"Thanks for helping me. Please call me Christian. Right now, I am no one's hope."

Ben did not like to see Christian giving up. "Don't give up so easily. In the darkest days, a light can pierce through. Do not give up."

Christian seemed to light up a little as he felt his fighting spirit stir. "I remember my dad saying something like that when I was young. He talked about the Lord being the light and that darkness can never put it out. I will not give up." Christian turned his head away. "I caused the death of a few of my people because of the way I handled my anger and pain. I thought of myself only. I should have worked with the news that the king ordered the death of my parents and kept my composure."

Ben eyes teared. "We are human and make mistakes."

Christian turned to Ben. "Again, I remember my dad telling me about the Bible and mistakes." Christian paused for a moment. "I remember my dad telling me about the most important message in the Bible: You should love the Lord your God with all your heart and with all your soul, and with all your mind." Christian tried to move a bit. "Before I came back, I used to have another wristband that had the words *God loves me* embroidered on it. Something happened in my life that opened my eyes and took all the pain away from my heart. I let God's love in. Because of that, I felt I had a purpose to come back and free our people. Looks like I am not doing that well."

Ben put his head down because of his shame. Then he turned his head and looked at Christian. "You are still among us. God can make anything happen. Just stay strong and fight."

Christian looked around at the bowls of food. "Ben, you need to stay strong as well and eat as I do. I figured out that you gave me your portion of food and water when I was so weak."

The two prisoners heard Brutus enter the dungeon and approach their cell. "A soldier told me you have eaten and you have been talking. That was a good show you put on for us." He smirked. "I think we are going to continue that for a while till it sinks in with the people that there is no Hope. They are under someone's control." Brutus paused; his expression was serious. "Do you want to tell me where King William's soldiers are headed?"

Christian felt hope because he now knew that the men had got away. His heart was comforted in that knowledge. "I have no idea," he told Brutus. "I just told them to leave and ride right away. So, you have not caught up with them yet?"

Brutus stood tall. "In time, we will get them. You may have helped give them a little extra time to live, but I promise you that the soldiers I sent after them will take care of them." Brutus looked at Ben. "Ben, how is Christian's back coming along?"

Ben looked back at him in disgust. "It is not bleeding anymore, but you can see how raw the skin is."

Brutus said, "We will give him a little more time to heal. Then we will do it again. I will let you know when we get those soldiers. Maybe they can join you." He looked right at Christian. "That would be something to see. It would put fear in the hearts of many people." Brutus looked at Christian's right wrist and focused on the wristband. "Did you find some inner peace finally to believe that God loves you? With all that you have been through, do you still feel that God loves you? Look at where you are! Look at what you have done! I heard about what you did when you were away … the men you killed with no mercy. Do you believe that God still loves you? He did not protect you from me. You are on your own and will die like that." Brutus turned and left the cell.

Ben turned to Christian. "God does not leave us. It is we who leave God. God wants us to be with him. I know that taking another life is a sin. I know you fought in the arena. You did not have much choice. God's people fought to survive, and right now we do need a savior."

Christian lay quietly on the straw. "I did lose my way when I was in the arena. I forgot everything my dad taught me. I enjoyed what I was doing. I am ashamed of myself, and it is hard for me to forgive what I have done. I know the Lord can forgive my sins, but it is so hard for me to forgive myself. I know God is above me. I just remember and do not let go."

Ben touched his hand. "Find your peace with God. Remember God is just, and there is no other like him. No one is above Him. You are still alive and here with us. God may still have a purpose for you. Your people need someone to fight for them and lead the way."

Christian struggled but managed to get on his knees to pray. "God, please forgive me of my sins and transgressions. Good people have died trying to help me. Please be with them and their families. My people and I need you. Please help us. I am just a man, and I know I cannot do great things without your blessing. I love you, Father." Christian lay down and fell asleep.

***

Crispin looked back at the soldiers who were following them, and he rode up to Curtis. "Curtis, it looks as if we've lost half of the soldiers who were tracking us." Crispin was a stout man but strong. He was good with the bow from horseback. The other twelve men were the closest thing he had to a family.

Curtis had everyone stop and look back at Brutus's soldiers. Alexander looked up at the sky and around them. "The trail we are on has turned east. I think they are trying to cut us off." Alexander came from a good family. His parents felt pride when he was asked to be one of the king's personal soldiers. He felt honored and was a skillful combatant.

Curtis turned toward him. "Any idea when they will be upon us?"

"I do not know."

Curtis looked at the men. "I need ten volunteers. We need to find a bend where our followers cannot see us. There we will dismount. We will wait in the woods with our bows and arrows ready. The remaining three of you will continue riding, leading our horses so it looks as if we are all still running."

Joseph spoke. "Curtis, I think you should keep on riding one of the horses. It is easy to tell who you are when you are riding."

Curtis took this in because he knew he rode tall in the saddle. "I hear you. Let's get this done. Dusk will come soon, and that would be the best time to attack."

They rode on until Joseph spotted a bend in their path. "Right there looks like a good spot."

"I agree with you," Curtis replied. He turned and addressed the ten chosen archers. "Take your capes off and tie them around the necks of your horses. Let's block this trail off. After that is done, find a spot in the woods. Each of you should pick a target. We will keep on riding and come back for you."

Curtis and the other two soldiers resumed their journey, leading the riderless horses. After an hour of riding, Curtis stopped. "Let's turn back. Dusk is upon us, and Brutus's soldiers should have reached that bend by now."

***

Joseph was one of the ten who had stayed back. The ten soldiers waited in a line spread out a little. Joseph said, "Here they come, men!" Soon Brutus's soldiers were upon them. Joseph and his men started shooting arrows at them. As one of Brutus soldiers yelled "Ambush!" his companions started to fall off their horses after being struck by arrows. Others ran into the barricade that had been made. After the first few arrows had been shot, Joseph and his men ran toward the soldiers continuing to shoot more arrows at them. The soldiers continued to fall to their deaths until only a few remained. Swords were drawn. One of Brutus's soldiers was able to slash Alexander on his side, and he fell. The soldier was ready to strike Alexander again but was struck by Joseph's sword. Joseph bowed down over Alexander and looked at his wound. "Cassian!

Come over here and help Alexander." Cassian was the closest to a medic they had. He was well known in their village because he had helped a lot of people. Cassian took over from Joseph. Joseph then stood up. "Everyone else, let's clear the dead bodies and throw them in the woods. Clear the debris from the trail. Take their swords and armor and pile it over here. I will collect the horses." After this was done, Joseph went to Alexander and Cassian. "How are you doing, Alexander?"

It appeared that Alexander could barely move, but he said, "I am fine."

By this time, Cassian had removed Alexander's armor and shirt so he could examine the wound. "There is a cut here on Alexander's side that I am worried about. It is a little too deep to heal on its own. I will need to stitch it up. We should do this before we move him."

Other men come over. "What do you need?" asked Joseph.

Cassian grabbed his bag, "I have everything I need here to do this. I will need help holding him down." Cassian sterilized the needle and thread with alcohol. He then poured more alcohol on the wound and started to sew Alexander's wounds. In a short time, Cassian finished and bandaged up the wound.

Cassian looked at Joseph. "I do not think he should ride. We need to make him a stretcher."

Joseph instructed others. "Take a few branches and make a stretcher. Connect it to two horses that we retrieved. I do not want to leave any strange tracks." With Joseph's help, the soldiers quickly assembled a stretcher and put Alexander on it. "Let's head in the direction Curtis went. They will find us. Keep your eyes open."

After an hour Cassian, yelled, "Riders in front of us!"

Joseph ordered the soldiers to change formation. "Prepare yourselves, men."

Cassian got a better look. "It's Curtis and the others."

Curtis approached them and saw the stretcher they had made. "How did it go?"

Joseph answered, "We killed all of them, but Alexander got slashed in the side. Cassian sewed him up."

Curtis got off his horse and approached Alexander. "How are you feeling?"

Alexander felt confident he was fine. "I will make it. The wound is dressed."

Curtis then got back on his horse. "We need to get off this trail. Let's head east now." He turned to the injured man. "Alexander, it might get a little rough, but that is only way to make it. We don't know where the other soldiers are."

Alexander remained still and said, "Lead the way."

They continued to travel for a few hours until they reached a gully. Curtis scanned the area. "This looks like a good spot to stay the night. Cassian, Crispin, and Joseph help me lower Alexander's stretcher. Arne, take care of the horses. Abel, get wood for a fire. Bard and John, get to the ridge of the gulley and stand guard." Arne was the youngest of them. He was very quick and willing to help with everything. Bard and John were brothers. They were total opposites but still were good men willing to fight for their country. The men lowered Alexander down and set the stretcher near the spot where Abel was building a fire. Once the fire was started, Curtis turns to Cassian. "How is Alexander's wound?"

Cassian looked at the wound. "I think he will make it. We just need to watch for infection. Alexander right now just needs to relax and get some sleep."

Alexander lay back and shortly fell asleep. The rest of the men continued check over their gear and supplies and took turns guarding the campsite. They did not know where the rest of Brutus's men were.

It was soon morning, and Cassian took another look at Alexander's wound. "It looks like your wound will heal, but you are going to have a scar."

Alexander smiled. "First one to have a scar because of combat. I will be fine."

Curtis checked with all his men to see how they were. "Let's finish eating and head southeast for a while. Let's try to find the old castle ruins." The men got Alexander's stretcher hooked up, and the party headed southeast. The weather turned on them after a while, so they stopped and made a shelter. They were concerned about Alexander getting a fever from his wound. After a few days, they started to head east. The men noticed what appeared to be a trail of people heading east.

Curtis stood up in the saddle and scanned the horizon. "Look over there. Does that look like a wall?" The soldiers looked at a long structure that was covered with vegetation.

Joseph said, "I think you are right, Curtis. And I think we are being watched."

Curtis looked for something white to tie to his sword but did not find anything, "Does anyone have anything white that I can attach it to my sword?" Alexander gave him a piece of fabric that Cassian had saved as a spare bandage. Curtis tied it to his sword. "Stay here, men, and I will go forward. Be ready to ride if something happens."

Joseph said, "We will not leave you. If something happens, we'll charge."

Curtis went forward. A man on horseback appeared out of nowhere and rode up to him. Curtis looked the man over. "My name is Curtis. I was sent to find these castle ruins by Christian. I was told that the leader of this place name is Edmund."

"I am Edmund. Why have you come here?"

Curtis seemed relieved. "We mean you no harm. We seek aid for one of our men who is badly hurt. I have horses and weapons I can trade—"

Edmund cut him off. "How did your man get hurt?"

Curtis leaned forward on his horse, becoming frustrated. "My men and I are being hunted by Brutus's men. We ambushed and killed half of them. There are a dozen more looking for us. This weather should have covered our tracks."

Edmund, chagrined, kept silent as he decided what to. Then he spoke. "How is Christian?"

"I do not know. We left right away. He told me he was going to confront the king because he found out he was the one responsible for murdering his parents."

Edmund turned his horse. "Bring your men in. Christian helped save the life of my son and our townspeople. Maybe you can help us as well. It is time my people learned how to fight." Edmund guided Curtis and his soldiers to the ruins. All Curtis saw was a group of makeshift tents. He did not see any solid structures at all. He noticed there was no easy way to defend this place. Edmund escorted the men to main tent, "Come into the tent, and I will get you some food and water. I will have someone help with your wounded man."

Curtis dismounted and addressed his soldiers. "Crispin, Cassian, and Joseph attend to the horses. The rest of you help me bring in Alexander. Then we'll bring in our weapons and supplies." As the men worked, Curtis approached Edmund. "Can you tell me where we are?"

Edmund led Curtis out of the tent and pointed southwest. "Christian told me we are a day's ride northeast of your kingdom. Because of the cliffs, you cannot go straight there from here."

Curtis smiled for he felt they were moving forward. "Tomorrow I am going to take a few of my men straight southwest to see if what Christian said is true. I am going to see if there is a way to get down the cliffs safely. Do you have any rope we could use?"

Edmund responded, "We do have some. I can have people start making some more."

"Good. The rest of my men will help you train your people to fight, keep guard, and help with work around here. We will do our part if you let us stay here."

Edmund was silent for a little. "I remember what happened when King William sent his men to destroy us. If Brutus is turning on men from his own kingdom, this village, by itself, does not have a chance. You and your men give us chance to defend ourselves."

The next morning, Curtis's men gathered to receive their orders. "Crispin and Cassian, you are going to come with me. We are going to head southwest to see if we can find a way to the castle. I have been told there is a cliff in the way that keeps people heading directly in that direction. It is over a day's ride. I want you to get provisions for us. Joseph, I leave you in charge of the rest of the men. I want you to help with work around here. Also help guard this place and train these villagers. Teach them how to fight. We are going to need them just as much as they will need us."

After Curtis, Cassian, and Crispin were ready to depart, Curtis approached Edmund. "I have left Joseph in charge of my soldiers and told him what to do. Go to him with what you need. We are leaving now."

Edmund replied, "I will talk with my people soon, and my aid will help with Alexander."

The three men mounted their horses and departed.

A COMMUNITY
BEGINS TO GROW

Edmund called all the villagers together. Once they had gathered, he addresses them: "Last night some of you were aware that soldiers from the kingdom had arrived in our temporary village. They tell us that the kingdom is now under the control of Brutus. He is the one who persuaded King William to attack us. Brutus is after these men as well. They were not among the soldiers who attacked our first village."

One of the villagers came forward and yelled, "Get rid of them! We do not need anyone else here. If we help these men, Brutus, will not be easy on us."

Edmund looked right at him. "Do you not remember what happened to our last village? One man saved us and sent us here. Brutus's soldiers are not going to have any mercy with us. These soldiers will help us fight and protect this place. We are all going to learn how to fight. You asked me to be the leader of this village. I tell you this—I do not see any other way. This strategy will give us a fighting chance for survival."

One of the villagers asked, "Where did those three soldiers go?"

"They went to see if they can find a shorter route to the kingdom."

The same villager said, "So they can bring more men here to finish the job? Get rid of them!"

"Do you think these soldiers need more soldiers to finish us off? They could have done the job already. Instead, they asked to help us. The same person who saved us saved them from being killed. Those three soldiers left to see if they could find out what happened to Christian. Whatever they ask, I will do to help them if they need my help to free Christian. My boy would not be standing here next to me if he had not intervened. I am not asking any of you to commit to helping me rescue Christian, but all of you will train and learn fighting skills. You will respect these soldiers and work with them. Do any of you object to my decision?" The villagers look upon each other. Although some still grumbled, none of them disagreed.

Edmund approached a female villager. "Luisa, I need you and your family to start making some rope. I do not know exactly how much yet, but it must be strong enough for a man wearing armor to use for climbing."

Luisa was almost nineteen years old. She was a hard worker and very spirited. She was strong and spoke her mind when she should not. Luisa clapped her hands together. "One thing I noticed about this place is that there is an abundance of natural materials that can be used for making a rope. I will get my family started. For what it is worth, I think you are right to help these men."

Just then, Joseph approached Edmund. Luisa glanced at Joseph, and their eyes met. Luisa left to meet with her family and let them know what they needed to do. Joseph thanked Edmund. "I heard your speech. Thank you. We will do our best to help in every way. What do you want us to do now?"

Edmund walked forward with Joseph. "Grab a few of your best swordsmen and archers. I will help them train my people. I met Christian before. I too was a gladiator at the same place where he fought in the arena. I too won many fights, but I watched him. I saw the bloodlust in his eyes. He had no mercy for anyone. I did not see myself winning a match against him. I was a free man seeking fame and fortune. I left and came to this country. I was surprised to see him at the last village, and I was surprised that he fought to save my people."

Joseph replied, "In the kingdom I am from, Christian respected everyone. He always helped the townspeople and looked out for them. Before the king took him as his son, the soldiers could do whatever they wanted. Something about him changed the king. Not all good things can last. Christian recently found out it was the king who ordered his parents killed. The king then took him in because of a myth that a boy with a mark on his wrist would help overthrow him. The king made this happen. Christian saved his life, and the king helped make him the killing machine he is. One thing I do know—if Christian is freed, the townspeople will help." Edmund and Joseph discussed what else needed to be done. Soon Edmund and a few of the soldiers began to train the villagers in fighting techniques.

***

The following day, Curtis, Crispin, and Cassian arrived at the ridge. Between the tops of the trees below they could see the castle far away. It looked different to them. They did not see many people out and about. Curtis said, "There she is, boys. I do miss home, but it does look different—there's just something about it." They looked at the cliff, which dropped down about thirty-five feet. The rock face of the cliff appeared to be solid. At the bottom of the cliff were two hundred acres of forest, and then there was a three-hundred-acre field between the forest and the castle walls.

Crispin grabbed a rope. "Well, what are we waiting for? Let's tie ropes around this tree trunk and head down."

Cassian replied, "Lead the way, Curtis. If this rope holds your weight, it will hold the rest of us for sure."

Curtis turned to Cassian and chuckled. "It's not my fault you don't have a great physique like mine! I will go down first." Curtis took off most of his armor before descending. When he reached the bottom, he looked around and called up to the men, "Come on down! It's clear."

After Cassian and Crispin had come down the rope, Crispin sized up the cliff. "The trip down was not that bad. It wouldn't hurt to set up a block and tackle so we could get people and equipment up and down faster and easier."

Curtis agreed. "That's a good idea. Let's head to the edge of the forest."

Once they got close to the edge of the forest, they saw several people collecting wood. They remained hidden, and Curtis asked, "Do you guys recognize any of these people?" Cassian and Crispin looked at the people and said they didn't recognize any of them. Cassian then removed his outer clothes so he would look more like a villager than a soldier. He put a little mud on his face. When Curtis realized what he was doing, he said, "Be safe." Cassian walked into the woods and approached one of the people collecting wood. They greeted each other, and then Cassian asked, "Can you tell me about the village? I was in that last village that was destroyed by guards from there. I'm not seeking any retribution. I'm just looking for refuge since I don't have anywhere to go to now."

The man replied, "You don't want to go there. It's not safe. The man that led the attack on your village—Brutus— is now in charge. He does not show any mercy." A boy approached them and looked at Cassian as if he recognized him.

Cassian looks at him, "Can I help you, son?"

The boy smiled. "Dad, this is Cassian one of King William's personal soldiers." He turned to Cassian. "I was your stable boy."

Cassian knew the boy had figured him out. "I remember you, Benedict."

Benedict said, "Dad, he was always good to me. He is a good man."

The man looked at Cassian in disbelief. "I am Richard. What happened to you guys?"

Cassian replied, "Christian sent us away so we could live. He felt something was going to happen."

"Well, it did. Christian was thrown into the dungeon the day you left. Brutus took over. He had Christian brutally whipped in front of the townspeople and let his soldiers do what they wanted. Brutus is running the kingdom using fear to gain control. The people who tried to help Christian were struck down by arrows."

Cassian felt Richard's pain, and he felt compelled to help. He told Richard, "Gather up anyone who needs to find refuge from Brutus and his soldiers and bring them to this part of the forest. You must be selective about who you share this with. We will find a way to save Christian and restore our kingdom."

A smile came across Richard's face. "How many of you are alive?"

Cassian paused for he did not want to give Richard too much information. "We are strong together."

Richard stood up even prouder now that he could see hope. "I will let people know what you said to me. I will be careful." Each then went his own way.

Cassian went back to Curtis and Crispin and said, "Well, my plan worked for a little until his son approached me. He was our stable boy, Benedict. I learned that Christian is in the dungeon and has been whipped in public. Brutus is running village by fear."

Curtis replied, "We should head back and plan what we are going to do next."

Cassian said, "I am not leaving with you. I am staying here. I told him to let people know about me if they are seeking refuge from Brutus and the soldiers." Curtis looked at him sternly, but Cassian said, "They have killed people already who tried to help Christian when he was being whipped. The soldiers are allowed to do what they want and run the village by fear. I told him to be selective with who he tells."

Curtis calmed down and Crispin spoke. "Well, looks like I will stay here with you."

Curtis knew they were right. "When I get to the top of the cliff, I'll send rations of food and water down to you. Stay safe. I will be back in four to five days. I am going to bring up the rope until we get back." Cassian acknowledged him and understood why Curtis was doing that. They all then headed back to the cliff. Curtis climbed up the rope and lowered most of the rations to Cassian and Crispin.

***

After a day's ride, Curtis returned to the village. Joseph saw that Curtis was alone. "Where are Cassian and Crispin?"

Curtis got off his horse. "They decided to stay back. Go get the rest of the soldiers and Edmund." As Joseph went off to gather the people, Curtis noticed two people walking toward him, one person obviously helping the other. "Alexander, it is good to see you up! Well, men, we learned a lot on our expedition. Cassian approached a man who happened to be Benedict's father. He found out that they put Christian in the dungeon and have whipped him to increase fear among the villagers. People were killed who tried to help Christian. Brutus is in charge and lets his soldiers do whatever they want." Curtis took a breath. "Cassian told them that, if anyone needed to find refuge, they should gather in the forest and meet with him. So, Edmund, our own townspeople might be joining us here. They will contribute to your village, and we will be glad for their help when we attempt to rescue Christian."

Edmund nodded and said, "What do you need?"

Curtis responded, "We will need multiple ropes, a few of them at least seventy-five feet long. Plus a few block and tackles to make it easier going up and down the cliff. We will need rations of food for those men." Curtis addressed his soldiers. "Men, we will need to rotate watch shifts so we can patrol this place, the kingdom grounds, and the top of the cliff. There should be two people at the top of the cliff, two people here to help train these villagers and new people who come, and two people to watch our kingdom's grounds. There should be four soldiers to help watch the grounds here. The rest will help here, and we will rotate responsibilities. When you are at the cliff, no rope will be left down. That will be our main defense." The soldiers acknowledged Curtis's orders, and he continued, "I told Crispin and Cassian that I would be back in four or five days. Joseph, I want you to figure out a rotating schedule. Edmund, if you have anyone to help us in forest below the cliff to watch the castle grounds, that would be helpful."

Edmund responded, "I can spare some of our people."

Curtis and Joseph continued to talk with the soldiers. They started to get things ready. Joseph went to check on the rope that was being made. As he approached Luisa's family's tent, he saw Luisa outside. This time their eyes met and locked. Joseph became a little nervous, and he said, "Are the ropes ready?"

Luisa moved a little to the side as Joseph watched. "What happened to a simple hello or how are you?"

Joseph acknowledged he had been too direct. "You are right. All I know is how to be a soldier and be direct."

Luisa gave him a big smile. "That is something that we will have to fix."

Joseph started to turn skittish because he didn't know what to do. "I am nervous enough. Right now, I need to check on those ropes."

Luisa blushed a little and smiled. "Come on in. We'll see how things are going." Luisa ushered him into the tent to meet her family. "This is my mom, Roxana, my father, Albert, and my little brother Jesse. Mom and Dad, this is Joseph, one of the soldiers who have come here." They all greeted each other.

Roxana said, "My daughter is right—you are handsome."

Luisa blushed even more and looked at her mom. "Mom, can you stop?" She turned to her father. "Dad, Joseph has come to ask how the ropes are coming."

Albert brought a length of rope forward. "This rope is about sixty feet long so far."

Joseph picked up the rope and tested its strength. "That is some good work. We will need it to be seventy-five feet long, and we will need one more besides this one. Also a few that are fifty feet long."

Albert said, "No problem. We can get this one finished tomorrow and start on the next one."

"That's great. Do you know how to make a block and tackle?"

"I do, and I can get started on that as the rest of the family finish the ropes. I will have that ready tomorrow as well."

Luisa escorted Joseph out of the tent. He paused and said, "I will see you in tomorrow."

Luisa smiled and said, "Yes, tomorrow."

As Joseph walked away, Luisa entered the tent and said, "Mom, thanks."

***

Three days passed, and Alexander was able to move around better. He approached Curtis and said, "I want to come with you. I want to be of value, and I don't want to stay here."

"Get ready then. You will ride in a stretcher. Cassian is there and can check you over." Curtis addressed Joseph as he began to assemble the supplies he would need. "Joseph, I am going to take John, Alexander, Abel, and Bard with me." He then addressed Edmund. "Joseph will oversee my men. If you need anything, go to him. Thanks for all your help." They reassembled Alexander's stretcher, mounted up, and took off for the cliff.

The group arrived at the clifftop late at night. Curtis said, "We'll make camp here. I don't want to go down the cliff in the dark. I don't know what's going on down there, and I don't want to take any chances."

Morning came soon enough, and the men threw the ropes down the cliff. Curtis spoke to John and Abel. "Alexander and Bard are going to come down with me. Abel and John, I want you to set up this block and tackle with this rope. Tie a knot every two feet in this rope. That should make it easier to climb." Abel got to work.

Curtis, Alexander, and Bard climbed down the cliff and made their way forward to where Curtis had last seen Cassian and Crispin. Once they get close, they noticed about fifteen people besides their own men. Curtis called out, "Cassian, are you there?"

Cassian came forward, obviously relieved. "Here I am."

Curtis, Alexander, and Bard walk toward Cassian and Crispin. The five men greeted each other. Cassian grabbed Alexander by the arm. "I am glad to see you back on your feet, Alexander. As you can see, some of our people are seeking refuge. You will recognize some of them."

Curtis looked around and did recognize some of the people. He did not see a threat in any of them. "I didn't think people would show up," he said. "Any word on Christian?"

Cassian replied, "No one here has seen him. He is still in the dungeon from what I hear. I have not seen any changes at the castle grounds either."

Curtis said, "We will have to get our people back to the camp. John and Abel are setting up a block and tackle system for those who cannot climb the knotted rope. Cassian and Crispin, I will have you come back with me while Alexander and Bard stay here to stand watch."

Cassian spoke up and said, "I will stay and keep a watch."

Alexander stepped forward. "I will stay here with him."

Curtis replied, "That's fine. We have some provisions for you."

Cassian said, "Our people have been bringing us supplies daily. Leave just a little."

Curtis acknowledged him and got the people ready to head to the camp. "You two stay safe." Then he addressed the assembled group of people. "All right, people, let's head to the camp where we have been staying. It is a day's ride away on horseback, so we have a little trip ahead of us. I will send a rider out to bring a wagon to come back."

Alexander turned to Cassian. "Thanks for helping me when I was wounded."

Cassian replied, "We are family, and that is what we do."

Curtis, Crispin, Bard, and the townspeople headed to the cliff. When they arrived, Crispin called up to Abel. Abel lowered the rope with the block and tackle.

Curtis yells up, "I have fifteen of our people coming up to you. Send down the other rope." A few men and young kids took turns climbing the rope up the cliff. Once all of them got up, Curtis spoke to John and Abel. "That worked great! We are going to leave here. You have your provisions. Cassian and Alexander are down there. Be aware of what happens down there. Someone will come to relieve you guys in four days."

The group of refugees headed toward the encampment; Crispin rode ahead to the camp.

When Crispin arrives at the camp, he sought Joseph and said, "Curtis and Bard are bringing back fifteen of our people. I want to send someone with the wagon to bring them here."

Joseph seemed happy. "Let's get it ready. I'll talk with Edmund in the morning. Take some extra horses with you." Once they got the wagon ready, Crispin left with two additional men, one to drive the wagon and one to manage the extra horses.

By midday Curtis, Bard, and Crispin arrived back at the camp with the fifteen refugees. Joseph and Edmund greeted them. Joseph recognized a few of them and addressed one of them. "Glad to see you, Ansel. I see you brought your whole family."

Ansel replied, "I am happy to see you as well. Things are not good in our kingdom. The guards are wreaking havoc on our people. I did not see any way to keep my family safe."

Joseph said, "We do expect you and your family to help with daily responsibilities here."

Ansel smiled. "That will be no problem."

"Everyone will be trained in fighting techniques," replied Joseph. "We need to keep ourselves safe. We are planning to take our kingdom back."

Ansel nodded. "Do you have a blacksmith and a woodworker here?"

Edmund said, "We have one blacksmith, but he could use help. And we have no woodworkers."

Ansel boasted a little. "Well, you are in luck, because those are the trades of my family." Edmund smiled. He had started the other village because he wanted to be part of a community, and he felt safer with their numbers growing. This time he was more assured they would make it.

Joseph and Edmund made sure the people were fed and provided with shelter. The men kept on rotating responsibilities. More and more townspeople come to their encampment. During this time, Joseph and Luisa had become fond of each other. The people continued to train and make weapons, especially much-needed arrows. They continued to keep a watchful eye because they knew Brutus's soldiers were out there still looking for them.

ONE MORE ROUND

It had been three weeks since Christian had endured a whipping. His wounds had begun to heal, but he had become weaker because of malnutrition. His appearance had declined, yet his demeanor was still positive. He focused on his faith in God. He still believed there was hope.

Brutus entered the dungeon and walked straight to Christian's cell. "How are you doing Christian?" he asked sarcastically with a big smile on his face.

Christian responded in a serious manner. "I am fine, but we know you do not care."

Brutus took a step back. "Now, I am offended by that. But we are going to have a great day. Today you are going to put on another show." Christian walked forward; he did not cower. Brutus continued, "You are anxious. I need to instill fear into the townspeople. It seems that people have been running away. No one is talking. They are keeping the identity of the helper's secret." Christian smiled a little. Brutus ordered the guards to put him in shackles and bring him out. Christian did not fight back; he even kept a smile on his face.

One of the soldiers said, "Looks like we'll have to be hard with that whip to take that smile off your face."

Brutus replied, "Now, we do not want to kill him. We still need him around, but you can hurt him." Christian was then taken out to the castle grounds. When the townspeople saw him, they started to walk away, but soldiers kept them from retreating. One of the soldiers blew a bugle to get the people's attention. Christian was secured in the pillory.

Brutus came forward and stood in front of Christian. "People, are you ready for another show? I want you all to pay attention because I hear people have been leaving our loving community. No one has told me anything at all about it. I want you to pay attention to what happens if you cross me." Brutus signaled the soldier with the whip, and he began to strike Christian. Every strike seemed to go deeper and deeper, tearing into his flesh. The townspeople were motionless and fearful of what was going on. The soldier continued to strike. Christian slumped in the pillory but managed to stand back up. Brutus saw this and said, "Are you ready to give up, Christian? Do you want mercy?" Christian just looked at him and smiled. Brutus said, "Whip him a few more times." After the soldier gave Christian several more stripes, Brutus held up his hand to stops it. "Now, my people—yeah, you are my people … I own you people—your fate will be the same as Christian's if you do not start telling me what is going on with the missing people!"

Brutus then noticed a beautiful woman in the crowd. He approached her and said, "What is your name?"

The woman answered reluctantly, "My name is Elizabeth. This is my husband."

Brutus looked the man over. "You can do much better than him. He is just a farmer. Come with me."

Elizabeth moved closer to her husband. "I have to deny my king," she whispered.

Brutus smirked, "I do not think I am going to give you a choice." Elizabeth's husband's demeanor changed. He stepped up to Brutus. Brutus took out his knife and sliced the man's throat in front of Elizabeth. Blood gushed out as the man fell to the ground. Brutus, enraged, addressed the crowd. "Do not ever think I am not your lord. Any of you! Your fate will be just as his was." He turned to the stunned woman. "Now, Elizabeth, it seems you are not married anymore. You are coming with me. I hope you get your mourning done by the time I get you to my chambers." He turned to his men. "Soldiers, take Christian back to the dungeon." Brutus grabbed Elizabeth roughly by the arm and took her away. The soldiers continued to be rough with Christian as they returned him to the dungeon. Once Christian was in his cell, Ben started to take care of him. "Don't worry. You are back with me in the cell. I am going to take care of you."

Christian relaxed as much as he could. "I know you will take care of me. I am just going to take a little nap."

Ben started to tear up a little when he took a closer look at Christian's back. He prayed, "God, I ask you again to help me. For, with you, I can get things accomplished." Ben first cleaned the wounds. Then he dressed them with the material he had.

The next morning, Elizabeth was allowed to leave the castle. She ran to her brother's house. She was greeted by her sister-in-law, Agatha, who invited her in. She noticed that Elizabeth was distraught, so she ushered her to a chair. "What can I do to help you?" she asked.

Elizabeth started to shake and rock back and forth in the chair nervously. "I need to see my brother."

Agatha responded, "He is out on guard right now. He will be back in an hour. Is there anything I can help you with or get you?" Elizabeth shook her head and continued to rock back and forth. Agatha tried to comfort her, but Elizabeth pushed Agatha away aggressively. "No, I just need to see my brother. I am going to just wait here."

Agatha slowly reached for her hand. "I am going to stay with you until he arrives. We do not need to talk, but I want you to know you are not alone." An hour passed, and Elizabeth's brother, Alec, returned home. When Alec saw his sister rocking in the chair, he looked at his wife, but she shook her head because she did not know what was wrong with her.

Alec walked to Elizabeth's side. "What is the matter sister?"
Elizabeth raised her head to him. "I need you to kill Brutus.
I need you to go do it right now." Alec could not believe his sister
would be asking him to do this. Elizabeth then said, "Kill King
Brutus."

Alec asked, "Why do you want me to do this?"

Elizabeth stopped rocking, and tears came down her face.
"Brutus killed my husband in front of everyone. Then he took me
to his bed chamber and raped me repeatedly all night long."

Alec was filled with rage. He stood and started to reach for his
sword, but Agatha stopped him. "Do not even think you are going
to try and kill Brutus. You will be killed, and your sister and I will
both be widows. We have two children, and I need your help raising
them."

Alec continued to move toward his sword. "I must," he said, and
he stood up ever so proudly.

Agatha said, "If you get killed, your children and I will be out on
the street, and nothing will stop Brutus and his soldiers from hurting
us. You need to come up with a different plan to keep us all safe."

Alec paused for a short time, thinking of what to do. "We will
leave and join the other townspeople who have left the village."

Agatha replied, "Are you sure that is a good idea? After all, you
are one of Brutus's soldiers. Maybe they will want to kill you as a
traitor."

Alec said, "I have always respected everyone and not taken
advantage of anyone. I do not see any other way. The way people
talk here, they will soon figure out Elizabeth is my sister, and Brutus
will see me as a threat. Brutus knows I will not forgive him."

Agatha shook her head. "We must do something else. You do
not know where these people are going."

Alec said, "We will have to find them. Listen, none of us is
safe here. When we get to this new encampment, I will ask for
mercy. If they kill me, you and the kids will be safe. You will be
with Elizabeth." They looked at each other and came to a silent

agreement. Alec said, "Do not tell the kids, but we will be leaving at nightfall." Alec paused and looked at Elizabeth, "My children are going to be here soon. You need to stay strong, so they do not see anything wrong. I do not want them to say anything about what is going on or what we have planned. Let it be a normal day for them."

Soon, Alec's kids come back to the house to get something to eat. They greeted their aunt, grabbed some bread and cheese, and headed back out to play. They had no idea what was going on or what was going to happen.

Night fell soon enough. Alec had been getting things ready. The children were sleeping. "Get everyone up," he said to Agatha. "It is time to go. All we need is what we are wearing and my weapons." Alec then turned to Elizabeth calmly and said, "Sister, I am so sorry that all this has happened to you, but I need you to continue to be strong. I need to get us out that gates."

All of them left the house. Alec walked down the side of the street while the rest of them tried to hide in the shadows behind him. He checked in every direction before they moved forward. So far, no one had detected them. When they finally reached the gates, Alec told them to stay back. As he approached the gates, he looked around and saw only three guards, one above the gates and two in front of the gates. "How is it going tonight soldiers?" Alec asked casually.

"It is good, sergeant," one soldier replied.

Another soldier said, "What are you doing out here at this time?"

Alec sized them up. "I'm just out for a walk. Couldn't sleep."

The soldier sitting atop said, "I see you looking at the gates. The gates do not open by orders of King Brutus. I think you should leave." Alec nodded and walked away.

Once Alec was out of the guards' sight, he joined his family. He took his bow and arrow from his wife, who had been holding them for him, and he touched her softly on the face. He looked at his kids. With a smile he said, "Once I let this arrow go, we need to run for that gate. There will be no stopping."

Agatha shook her head. "I do not want to take the chance."

Alec said, "They know who I am, and it will be reported. They will figure it out." Alec looked at the guards and saw that they were not looking in his direction. He nocked an arrow in his bow, pulled the bowstring back, and released the arrow. It hit the soldier at the top of gates. He fell heavily in front of the other soldiers. Alec charged the two soldiers in front of the first gate. Both of them had their swords at the ready. The soldier on the right stepped forward and suddenly stabbed the other soldier in the stomach instantly killing him. Alec, by this time, was close to them, but he stopped suddenly. "Do I need to worry about you?"

The soldier wiped the blood from his sword. "I was going to kill this man at some point tonight. He raped the woman I am going to marry. He knew my intentions, but he still decided to do it."

Alec said, "You should come with us."

The soldier replied, "I cannot. I have family still here. They will suffer for my actions. I will let you out. This is what you need to do, Alec." Alec looked at him harder. The soldier said, "Yes, I know your name, and I know what Brutus did. Find a woman named Emma tell her Charles sent you. My betrothed's name is Emma. She has already left. She asked me to join her, but I could not. Run to those woods. Be close to your wife and kids. But first, I need you to cut me with your sword and then knock me out." They opened the gates. Alec cut Charles on his side and knocked him out with his sword handle.

The fleeing group cautiously make their way to the woods. Alec grabbed his wife's hand and his son's hand. He told his daughter to hold her brother's hand. "We need to stay together. If they find me by myself, I may lose my life." Agatha looked at him in alarm. Alec said, "We have no choice now. Keep on going."

When they finally made it to the woods, Alec felt as if someone was watching him. They moved deeper into the woods. Suddenly, men appeared around them with bows up. Alec started to speak, but he was interrupted.

A voice said, "I know who you are. I know you train Brutus's soldiers. I might spare your family, but not you."

Alec replied, "Brutus raped my sister and killed my brother-in-law. I want nothing more to do with him."

The voice said, "We will let your family join our encampment."

Alec replied, "That is all that matters to me. I want them to be safe."

The voice said, "Who does your allegiance lie with?"

"I may be a soldier, but I never harmed anyone. Not until tonight. I killed one of Brutus's soldiers at the gates."

The person who had been speaking motioned to the others to lower their bows, and he stepped forward. Alec recognized Cassian and said, "I see you have evaded Brutus's soldiers. That is good."

Cassian replied, "Our numbers are growing. Would you be willing to join our group?"

"If you are able to keep my family safe, I will help in any way." Cassian took Alec and his family to the other families that were waiting. When they got there, Alec asked Cassian if there was a woman there named Emma. Cassian called her over, and Alec spoke with her. "I saw Charles tonight. He helped us escape."

Emma got excited, "Is he alright? Did he come with you? Is he safe?"

"He killed the other guard who was with him. He did not come with us. He is worried what would happen to his family."

Emma's eyes start to get teary. "He did say that to me also, but I did not react as I should have because of what happened to me."

Alec did not know what to do. "I am sorry for what happened."

Elizabeth came forward and put her arm around Emma. "I was raped also," she said. I saw Charles kill the man who did it to you." They embraced each other and felt comfort in each other's arms. Cassian told them it was time to head to the base of the cliff. At that point, there were about seven people watching the castle grounds.

***

When morning came to the castle, Carl told Brutus what had happened at the gates the previous evening. Brutus threw his drink down in disgust. "The soldiers cannot even watch a gate! How incompetent are they?"

Carl replied, "This was not just any ordinary soldier. It was Alec who did this."

"I never expected him turn on us."

"From what I heard, it is related to that man you killed and the woman you took to your bed. The woman was his sister."

Brutus shook his head and got up. "I really know how to pick women, don't I?" He paced a little. "We will double our guards. If people find out that Alec left, we might have more defectors." Carl nodded in agreement. Brutus asked, "Have they found King William's personal soldiers?"

"I have not heard anything about them. It has been confirmed that we did lose half of our soldiers who had been looking for them. They split, and half were ambushed on the road."

Brutus became even more enraged. "I told them to stay together when they were in pursuit. I figured this would happen. Make sure they keep on looking for them."

"They will, Brutus."

***

Two days later, Alec and his family arrived at the encampment. Alec, who was still dressed as a soldier, caught everyone's attention. People started to get hostile toward him, but Curtis stepped in. "Stop! This man is here for the same reason you are."

One man yelled, "He is one of them!"

Curtis replied, "I know this man. Yes, he is one of them. He trained them. Can any of you tell me if he harmed you?"

A voice yelled again, "He is one of them!"

Curtis said, "The fact that he was with them is not a good enough reason to condemn him. No one can come forward and say he took advantage of anyone here. For that reason, he is going to stay with us. No harm will come to him or his family." Curtis looked at Alec. "Now that we have that addressed, Alec, one way you could help us is to work on training people on the use of the sword, the spear, and the bow." Alec agreed. Some of the people were disgruntled with this. Curtis looked at Edmund, "Edmund, can you show Alec what we have been doing?" Edmund and Alec walked off together toward the training field.

SECRETS CANNOT
BE KEPT

Weeks passed. At the encampment, as Alec helped train the people in combat techniques, they began to accept him and trust him. They saw him as a good man.

The love between Luisa and Joseph began to blossom. When Joseph was assigned to the perimeter guard by the wall, she would ride out to see him. One day, she rode out to Joseph and showed off to him on her horse. Joseph was not paying attention to the perimeter as he should have been. Suddenly, Crispin stood up and yelled, "Brutus's soldier just spotted us and took off! He must have seen Luisa on her horse!" Crispin jumped on his horse and went after the fleeing soldier.

Joseph told Luisa, "Go back to the camp. Tell Curtis and Edmund. I am going with Crispin." He then raced off.

Luisa rode her horse hard to the camp. She was frantic when she found Curtis. "Crispin and Joseph took off after one of Brutus soldiers. They went west. The soldier must have seen me ride my horse. This is my fault." Luisa turned her horse and took off after Joseph.

Immediately Curtis got people ready to help pursue the soldier. "Crispin, Joseph, and Luisa went after the soldier. Leave the heavy armor off. We need to ride light. Just bring your swords and bows.

I'm hoping that his horse is worn down. We need to head west. Keep your eyes open!" They took off as fast as they could. Edmund got other people to watch the perimeter.

***

Brutus's soldier ran his horse hard. Crispin knew he could see Crispin and Joseph behind him. Crispin could see he was closing the gap. Joseph had not caught up to them yet. Over one rolling hill after another, there was no change in his direction. The soldier just kept on riding west. Crispin continued to get closer to him. The soldier's horse was becoming fatigued as Crispin got closer. Soon they were on an open plain, and Joseph was slowly gaining ground on Crispin. They soon saw a tree line on the horizon and started to ride their horses as fast as they could. Crispin and Joseph soon were close enough to shoot an arrow at the soldier. Crispin shot an arrow and ended up hitting the horse on his side. The horse jumped a little. Joseph shot an arrow, hitting the soldier. The soldier fell off the horse and crashed to the ground. The horse kept on riding west. Crispin pursued the horse while Joseph checked on the soldier. The soldier was dead. Joseph got back up on the horse and went after Crispin again. Soon the horse made it to the tree line. Crispin was close behind it. Crispin pushed his horse harder and harder so he could catch up to the horse. He was unaware of what he was heading into, but he knew he needed to get that horse before it reached the location where Brutus's soldiers were. He didn't want the soldiers to see his arrow on the side of the horse because then they would know in what direction they should head to find the encampment.

The riderless horse started to pant hard but made it over a small bluff. Crispin heard a voice say, "Whoa!" Once he got near the top of the bluff, he jumped off his horse and ran to the top with his bow in hand. He saw one of Brutus's soldiers grab the reins of the horse. Immediately, Crispin let an arrow fly. It hit the soldier in the neck, killing him. Another of Brutus's soldiers who had seen this yelled,

"We are under attack!" He charged toward Crispin, who shot an arrow at him, but the soldier blocked it with his shield. Crispin saw another man coming out of a tent. The path was clear, so Crispin let an arrow fly, and again he hit his target. The soldier with the shield was soon ready to attack Crispin. Crispin could hear Joseph's horse coming over the bluff, so he ran north of the soldier with his sword in hand. The soldier turned toward Crispin. When Joseph cleared the bluff, he saw the soldier and struck him down instantly.

Crispin was exhausted. "What took you so long?" he asked, panting.

Joseph cleaned off his sword. "I made it just in time. You are still intact."

Crispin smirked. "You let Luisa distract you. Thankfully, we found them before they found us." Joseph shrugged a little for he knew Crispin was right. Crispin said, "Now there are only eight men out there looking for us."

Joseph replied, "We need to get rid of these bodies and extra horses." Joseph and Crispin heard an approaching horse, so they got ready to strike, but suddenly Luisa came up the bluff riding frantically. She rode straight to Joseph and got off her horse. This angered Joseph, and he said, "You know you almost got killed. You cannot be doing this." Luisa saw how angry Joseph was, and she started to sob. Joseph softened his voice and said, "I Love you. Do you think I want to see you get killed?"

Luisa smiled and started to control her tears. "You love me? That is the first time you have said it."

"We can talk more about it later. We need to clear this up."

Crispin said, "Joseph, let's take the uniforms from those two and place those bodies in that tent." He turned to Luisa and said, "Keep your eyes open for other soldiers." Crispin and Joseph worked to hide the bodies.

Ten minutes later, Curtis rode over the bluff along with other villagers. They saw the tents, and he said, "Looks like you guys were busy. What is the plan?"

Crispin replied, "Joseph and I will dress up in their gear and we'll wait for them. I figured a few of our people can be in the trees over here and two others in the trees there." He pointed to the nearby trees at the edge of the forest. "When they come close to the fire, we can start attacking. Someone needs to take the extra horses away."

Joseph looked at Luisa. "I need you to take the extra horses and equipment back to the camp and stay there."

Luisa looked at Joseph and smiled in agreement.

Crispin removed the arrow from the injured horse and tied the animal up with the other horses. It was a small wound and would soon heal. Luisa left with four horses. Curtis and Alec rode with her to the edge of the woods. Curtis said, "Have a safe ride back to the camp. When you get to the river, stop for a little bit so the horses can get some water."

Luisa turned slightly to them, "I will. Take care and be safe." She rode away.

As Alec and Curtis watched, they saw one of Brutus's soldiers appear from a different section of the woods. The soldier did not charge after her, but he stayed back, constantly looking behind him making sure he was not being followed. Curtis got ready to charge, but Alec put his arm in front of Curtis to stop him. "He does not see us. Get off your horse."

"She is in danger."

Alec said, "Our horses will not catch up to him. We rode them hard here." Curtis realized that he was right. Both got off their horses. Alec said, "He is not looking to kill her. He wants to follow her. Look at how he is acting. He has not seen us yet. When he gets over that ridge, we will ride there." Curtis nodded in agreement but was upset because he was used to charging. Alec continued, "A good place to get him would be at the river."

The soldier was now between Luisa and Curtis. He kept looking back, but Alec and Curtis knew he could not see anything behind him. Once the soldier went over the ridge, Alec and Curtis followed him quietly on horseback. Alec dismounted and ran to the ridge so

Hope Is it on Time

he could see where the soldier was. After locating the soldier, Alec ran back to his horse and told Curtis, "We are gaining on him." They headed over the bluff, and Curtis got a glimpse of the soldier; they were gaining on Brutus's man.

Curtis said, "We have one more ridge to gain on him without being seen. After that, it is open ground a little before we get to the river where there are trees for cover. Let's close that gap even more." Curtis and Alec rode hard to the next ridge.

***

Back at the camp, Joseph and Crispin were wondering where Alec and Curtis were. Joseph said, "They must have gotten into some type of trouble or would have been back by now."

Crispin replied, "Luisa will be fine. Curtis will make sure nothing happens to her. Let's keep this fire going." Crispin left to walk down the path to get some wood for the fire. When he was out of Joseph's sight, one of Brutus's soldiers called out to him. Crispin gathered some logs and walked back to the fire as if he had not heard the soldier. Soon an arrow shot out from a tree, hitting the soldier knocking him off his horse. Crispin ran to the soldier with his sword and finished him off. He was looking over the body as Joseph approached him. Crispin then said, "This does not come easy. I knew this man."

Joseph walked over to Crispin and grabbed the man's arm. "He was ready to kill you. What choice did you have?" Crispin was still shaken, but he nodded. Joseph then said, "Now help me dispose of the body." They moved the body into the tent while other villagers kept an eye out for anyone approaching.

***

Alec and Curtis continued to pursue the soldier who was following Luisa. Neither Luisa nor the soldier looked back at any point to see if they were being followed. Soon Luisa was at the river.

She leaned forward and rubbed her horse's neck, "Good job, Lady. Now let's get some water." She got off her horse and let all the horses drink water. She was relieved to have made it that far safely. She walked into the river a short way, bent down, gathered some water, and splashed it over her face and arms. She had no care. At no time was she aware that she was being watched. She stood up and looked back at the horses. Now she started to get nervous because she got a glimpse of something that did not belong there beyond the horses. She did not know exactly what she had seen, so she started to walk to her horse. The soldier came from behind the trees and walked toward her, but he was having a hard time walking. She stood frozen still. The soldier continued to advance, but he went from tree to tree, leaning heavily on each one as he progressed. Luisa soon noticed an arrow protruding from the soldier's back. Suddenly, she heard horses coming toward her. Curtis appeared out of nowhere with his sword in hand and struck the soldier down, sending him to his death.

Curtis came to her with Alec trailing behind him. "I am glad you are safe, but you need to realize there are powerful people who want us dead. You need to be aware of your surroundings."

Luisa nodded her head. Her entire body was shaking. "Thanks."

Alec approached them and said, "Now that was teamwork. Good shot with your arrow!"

Luisa said, "Hi. How long was he following me?"

"He has been following you since you left the woods," Curtis replied.

"What took you both so long?"

Curtis responded, "He was watching behind him until he himself felt he was not being followed. We would not have been able to chase him down before he got to you."

Luisa seemed to understand, but she was still in shock at what happened. She thought for a moment and then responded, "What about the other men we left at the camp? Should you not be with them?"

"We just saved you and others by preventing this soldier from

finding out where our encampment is. Is that not good enough?"
Curtis said.

Luisa became fierce. "You need to leave now and go be with
them!" She was thinking about Joseph.

Curtis said, "It is too late to head back there now. They might
not be able to recognize us in the dark."

Luisa replied sternly, "I am going to head back."

"No, you are not. I am not having you risk my men's lives
because of the twinkle you have in your eye for Joseph." This
obviously bothered Luisa, and Curtis said, "You told us the soldier
got a glimpse of you when you were showing off on your horse by
the wall for Joseph."

Luisa calmed down some. "What are we going to do then?"

Curtis replied, "We are going to head back to our encampment.
But go slowly when we get near it. We don't want anyone to get
hurt." They agreed. Curtis added, "Finish watering the horses. I'll
get the soldier's equipment to take back to the camp." When they
were ready, they started back to the camp and arrived just at dusk.
Curtis spoke with Alec, "Take care of the horses and the soldiers'
equipment. I'm going to find Edmund and let him know what is
going on."

Curtis found Edmund walking to his tent. "Edmund!" Curtis
called out. Edmund stopped and looked back as Curtis approached.
"We found where they were meeting," reported Curtis. "Five of them
have been killed. I have men at their camp waiting to ambush them."

Edmund replied, "Why did you not stay there with them?"

Curtis said, "Alec and I noticed a soldier tracking Luisa on her
way back to camp. We caught up to him before he could get to her.
By that time, it was too late to head back to their camp. Going back
would endanger them and myself. I didn't know when those soldiers
would return."

Edmund sighed. "What about our encampment here?"

Curtis replied, "As for now, it is safe. We brought back more
horses and equipment."

"At least our numbers are increasing, and it's good to have the additional equipment. If they do come, we should be able to defend ourselves."

"I do agree with you, but we need to keep training our people for that day."

"Until that day comes, we will train. Have you eaten anything yet?"

"No."

"Let's go and get something to eat."

***

At the enemy's encampment, Crispin and Joseph sat next to the fire they were careful to keep going. They prepared something to eat, and at dusk, they waited for more soldiers to come. Crispin noticed Joseph did not seem as focused as he usually was. "Boy, what's wrong with you? Love should make you strong, not like a little puppy."

Joseph replied, "I'm worried because Curtis has not returned. I've never felt about anyone the way I feel about Luisa."

"Have some faith that they are fine. I think I'm going to start calling you little puppy." Crispin laughed. Joseph laughed as well, and he cheered up a bit. Just then they looked up to see four soldiers on horseback enter their camp and come near the fire. One of Crispin's men called out to them, but they did not respond. Arrows started flying at the incoming soldiers. Joseph and Crispin attacked with their swords. A few soldiers fell after being struck by arrows; others involved Joseph and Crispin in sword fights. Suddenly, another soldier appeared and charged the camp with his sword up. One of the village people who had been hiding out in the trees shot him with an arrow. The soldier fell, his sword abandoned. After killing one of the other soldiers, Crispin charged after the soldier who had just arrived. He stabbed him and made sure he was dead.

One of the men came quickly down from his post in the trees and ran to Crispin. "There was another soldier with this man. He turned around right away and headed toward the castle." Crispin looked at Joseph and ran for his horse.

Joseph yelled, "Stop!"

But Crispin was already on his horse. "Why should I stop?"

"It is nightfall. We're not going to go out there blindly. We don't know exactly what's out there!"

"Aren't you concerned they may find us if we let him live?" Crispin asked.

"Yes, I am concerned. But I am not going to put anyone at risk. The good thing is it looked like he came from the south of this camp. That leaves all other directions from here."

Crispin got off his horse. "What should we do now?"

"Crispin, I want you to get those horses. The others will help me gather the soldiers' equipment," replied Joseph. They got to work, and when Crispin brought the horses to the camp, Joseph smiled and said, "At least we have enough horses now for everyone. If we didn't, Crispin, you would have to share your horse." Crispin and others laughed at the thought. They secured their equipment on the horses and mounted up. Joseph said, "We're going leave camp now and head northeast till we get to the river. We'll ride along the river till we get to the point turning east."

One of the villagers asked, "Why are we leaving now?"

Joseph replied, "I don't know if other troops are out there. I don't know if that soldier is going to double back. In the cover of darkness, we will leave this camp."

"Why not go straight east?" another man asked.

Joseph replied, "If the soldiers come back here and our tracks remain, they will see people have left this camp in two different directions."

They left the camp and rode all night. In the morning, they arrived at their encampment. Joseph and Crispin found Curtis and Edmund training people. Joseph and Crispin dismounted while the other men took their horses to the stable and stored their equipment in a tent. Joseph then said, "We got six more, but one got away in the darkness. What happened with you two?"

Curtis replied, "One was following Luisa. Don't worry—we got him first. Tell me about the one that got away."

"By the time we were alerted, he was gone in the darkness. It would have been difficult to track him, and I was not going to send anyone out there blindly. We don't know what's out there." Curtis did not question his decision because he knew it was the right one. Joseph said, "Our people are looking more like soldiers every day. We should be able to defend ourselves here if something happens."

Edmund replied, "I agree with you. Our people don't seem to be feeble anymore. They are feeling proud because they know they can defend themselves if need be."

Luisa saw Joseph and ran to him as he was talking. Joseph saw her and walked to her. "You are safe!" Luisa said. "I was so worried." Joseph then hugged and kissed her. Luisa asked, "Why did you not come find me first?"

"I love you, but the safety of this encampment must come first, and I needed to report to Curtis and Edmund and let them know what had happened."

"I don't understand that! I feel that I should be first," Luisa said.

Joseph replied, "If everyone is safe, I then know you are safe. Don't take it wrong. I am a soldier first. I do love you, and I was so worried not knowing what happened. Thank God you are okay."

Luisa blushed a little and embraced Joseph tighter. "When you say those words to me, I can always forgive you," she said. Joseph and Luisa walked together hand in hand.

After Joseph left, Edmund said to Curtis, "I am not happy that they did not go after that last soldier."

Curtis replied, "I hear what you're saying, but he has a point. If one of our people is captured, are you sure he or she will not say anything about where we are? I can tell you this—anyone captured will be tortured."

"I cannot answer that," Edmund replied.

Crispin, hearing this, came forward and said, "The soldier came from south of the camp. He had a good lead on us in the darkness. I was ready to chase after him, but I will not disagree with Joseph's decision to ride back here after nightfall. I could hardly see in front of me. Good thing the horse can see because I would not have known where to lead him."

Curtis interrupted, "Edmund I don't think we will need to worry about a lot of troops coming after us out here."

Edmund replied, "What makes you so confident about that?"

Curtis said, "Brutus sent twenty-four soldiers after us. Only one soldier is returning to him alive. Look at the people that have defected to us. Some of them were new soldiers there. Brutus's military force is decreasing, and I do not think he is going to send anyone else out to find us. He is going to keep his troops there because he fears we are going to come for him."

Edmund said, "I see your point and hope you are right." Curtis and Edmund returned to training the people as Crispin went to get something to eat.

BAD NEWS FOR BRUTUS

Three days later, the castle guards saw a soldier returning. One of them was sent to notify Brutus. He found Brutus talking to Carl. The soldier said, "Bertram is returning to the castle. He was one of the men sent to find those troops."

"One!" replied Brutus in a disgusted manner. They all headed to the castle grounds and arrived just as the soldier made it to the castle and almost fell when he dismounted because he was so exhausted. "Where are all of the other men?" demanded Brutus.

"They have all been killed by Curtis's men. I was the only one who escaped."

"How can this be? How were they able to do this?" Brutus said in disbelief.

"They were dressed in our clothing and armor, and they had posted men in the trees. I saw five of our men taken down right away."

Carl said, "Why did you not charge in?" His eyes were full of anger.

Bertram replied, "If I had charged in, I would be dead also, and I would not be able to tell you where we were at when they found us. One of them must have found their encampment."

Carl placed his hand on his sword. "Let's go and get some men."

Brutus faced him, "Stop!" He paused for a little. "We have lost twenty-three men going after them. They are now expecting us, and I am sure they are prepared. They must have gathered all the soldiers' equipment and taken their horses. People have defected from here—even some of our own soldiers. We will not share this information with anyone."

Carl shook his head. "I do not think we need to be weak and hide behind walls."

Brutus looked at him and spoke in a stern manner. "If we send out more troops and they come up dead, we might as well give them the castle. Some of the new troops we have now are not loyal to us. They are doing our bidding because of fear—fear that I will harm them or their families. We need to defend this place." Carl did not disagree with him and calmed down. Brutus then said, "Bertram, go get something to eat and get some rest. Carl, let's go to the dungeon and get Christian. I want him taken outside of the gates so they can see him from the woods. I feel they are watching us. I want them to see Christian being whipped. This time we will make him hurt more, so they will become angry. Hopefully that will get them to come after us. We will then be prepared."

Carl said, "I like how you think." Brutus and Carl headed to the dungeon to get Christian.

***

Christian was lying down in his cell, but he got up when he saw them coming. "Is it time already for me to take a walk?" he asked Ben, his cellmate.

Ben replied, "It has only been a little over three weeks."

Christian motioned to Ben to stop talking. He turned and addressed Brutus and Carl. "Something must have happened for you to come this early. Let me guess. All the soldiers you sent out must be dead."

Brutus replied, "I can see you still have your wits about you. We have an idea where they are, but I think it is better that they come to us." Brutus held his head high. "This show will be better than all the others. We are going to take you outside the castle grounds so they will see you from the woods. It will anger them, I am sure. I realize I have been doing this wrong. This will bring them out and force them to come to me. We will be ready."

Christian began to worry. Brutus said, "It looks like you are worried. Is it because you know that, when people focus on anger and allow themselves to be led by anger, they can make mistakes? If Curtis is leading them, they might do something rash. I am counting on it."

Brutus motioned to the soldiers. "Get Christian ready and make sure he cannot get out of the restraints. We are going to take a long walk out of the castle grounds." Carl had been smiling all this time. Christian and Ben did not say anything more, but worry was evident in Christian's eyes. He was not worried about himself; he was worried about others who might rush in to try to save him.

Once the restraints were put on Christian and he was led out of the dungeon, Brutus said, "Carl, do you have the bugle? You can blow it to announce to our townspeople that there will be an event of interest."

Carl reached in the folds of his tunic and pulled out the bugle, "I have it here, and I am ready. I only play it for special occasions."

Brutus grinned and looked at Christian. "That is what I like to hear. Play with all your heart."

Carl started to blow the horn. Christian shook his head as people cleared the roads and went somewhere else. None of the townspeople wanted to see what was happening. They didn't want to be around because of what had happened last time. They feared the soldiers even more than before.

"Pick up the pace, Christian," Brutus said. "You have gotten out of shape some, haven't you? We provide you with a good diet. Maybe you have just given up hope and are realizing your fate. This is good to see."

Christian did not reply to Brutus but realized he was right. He had not done any type of exercise and had lost a lot of muscle mass. He had started to lose faith that he would be rescued from the predicament he was in. After a bit, Brutus said, "No response from you. That is a change, and it is good. You finally see what your role is and what is expected of you."

Carl continued to blow the horn as they walked to the gate. People continued to flee in the other direction as they heard the horn being blown, but the sound attracted three boys who were outside the walls. The soldiers led Christian through the gate. Brutus looked around and saw a single pole resting on two upright poles. "Tie him to that pole. Make sure his arms are secured tight." The soldiers took Christian to the pole and forced him to spread his arms out. They then secured his arms in position.

"Are you feeling comfortable, Christian?" one of the soldiers said.

Christian looked to his left and right. Sadness overcame him, and he looked up at the sky. He said to himself, *Be with me, God, for I will need your strength to get through this. I cannot do this alone.* A little comfort came to him as Carl prepared to use the whip on him. The three boys were standing close to the soldiers. Carl yelled, "Here comes the first strike, Christian. I hope you are ready for it." Carl let the whip fly and intentionally missed Christian. Carl noticed Christian flinching at the sound of the whip. "I never thought I would see you tense up like that," he said. "You are not as strong as I once thought." Christian did not reply but kept silent. He knew what could happen. After the moment passed Carl said, "No response either. You must be becoming even more tame. Okay, Christian, here it comes."

Carl repeatedly struck Christian with the whip. The end of the whip dug deeper and deeper into Christian's back, drawing blood wherever it struck. The three boys watched. One of the boys picked up some stones and started to throw them at Carl. One hit him in the ribs. Carl yelled, "Get that boy and bring him to me!"

The boys took off running, and the soldiers pursued them. The boy who had thrown the stones was slower than the other two. Soon one of the soldiers was able to catch the boy. He started to drag the boy back to Carl. Carl continued striking Christian numerous times with the whip. Each strike left its mark, cutting into Christian's body. Christian slumped in his restraints but managed to get up. Carl yelled to him, "Glad to see you stand back up. I have a few more strikes for you."

Soon the soldier arrived with the boy. When Carl saw the boy, he smiled and continued to strike Christian. Christian was barely able to stand even though the whip, this time, did not seem to hurt as much as it had before. Christian had felt the initial strikes, but the sting did not stay with him even though there was blood all over his back.

Brutus looked at Carl with utmost satisfaction. "I think he's had enough. I am sure Curtis's men saw the show. This should make them angry." They both looked toward the woods. Brutus felt glorified. "Take him back to the dungeon."

Carl replied, "I have some other business to attend to. I will see you later." Carl grabbed the boy. "Take me to your father. If you do not, you will never see him again." One of the soldiers went with Carl as the boy struggled unsuccessfully to get away from Carl.

The boy took them to a small hut where a man was working outside. "Father!" the boy yelled. The man turned around. To Carl's surprise, he said, "Thomas." A smile came to Carl's face. "This must be my day because it's getting better and better."

Thomas looked nervous. "What do you want of my boy?"

"Your son was throwing stones at me, and now he has to pay the price," Carl said. He struck the boy with his hand.

Thomas took a step forward but then stopped himself. "I will take whatever punishment my son has coming."

Carl grinned even wider. "Thomas, I am going to enjoy this. Christian is not here to save you now." Thomas did not say anything at all. He knew that, if he struck back, he would be beaten to death or his son would be killed. Thomas knew who was in power. Carl said, "Go sit over there, boy, while I beat your father." Carl let go of the boy, and the boy sat down on a log. Thomas walked forward as the other soldier got behind him.

Thomas looks at his son. "Sit still and do nothing."

Carl now was in Thomas's face. "That is some good advice you have given him." Carl nodded at the other soldier, and they both struck Thomas, knocking him to the ground. He tried to get up, but they struck him down several more times. Tears streamed down the boy's face as he watched his dad being beaten. The boy got up and ran to his father, crying for them to stop. Carl put the boy back on the log and got ready to strike Thomas again.

In desperation, Thomas yelled, "Please stop!"

Carl lowered his fist. "I think Thomas has had enough, don't you think so? Let us leave him and head back to join the others." Carl looked at Thomas. "Control your son. If he throws stones at us again, we will be back again, and this time we will not be as nice."

As soon as Carl and the soldier had left, Thomas's son ran to him with tears running down his face. "I am sorry, Dad. They were whipping that man, and I had to do something to help him."

Thomas was in pain. "It's okay, my son. Give me a hug—gently—and help me to the hut." It was a struggle to get Thomas inside. He did not show any rage; rather, he showed understanding. "You are a good son, Henry. Even though this happened to me, you stood up for what is right. But, because of the soldiers' control here, we do have to watch what we do." Thomas managed to sit in a chair. Henry brought him some water. Thomas said, "I don't think any bones are broken. I am just going to take it easy right now."

Henry looked at his dad. "I am going to get some wood and get a fire going so we can make something to eat." Thomas looked at the fireplace, especially at the corner of the wooden mantel he had made. Henry said again, "Dad, I am going to get some wood."

Thomas, still looking at the corner of the mantel, replied,

"That is a good idea, son." Thomas got up and walked over to the mantel. He removed a small piece of wood that camouflaged a secret compartment. He looked inside and saw a sword—his sword. He remembered a moment in time when Christian had brought the sword to him. "A time may come that you need this, Thomas," Christian had said.

"I am not supposed to have any weapon," Thomas had responded. "You know what will happen if Brutus's soldiers find this."

Christian had replied, "Things might go in a direction no one wants. You will need to be able to defend yourself if danger comes. My parents did not have the skill or tools to defend themselves. You have the skill, and all you need is this."

"What if the soldiers find it?" Thomas had responded.

Christian had said, "You are a skilled woodworker. Hide it until you need it."

Thomas replaced the piece of wood, and the sword was once again hidden. Henry came back, his arms full of firewood. "Dad what are you doing over there? You should be lying down."

Thomas responded, "I will be fine, son. I'm just waiting for the warmth of the fire."

"I will get it going for you, Dad," Henry replied.

When the fire was blazing and Thomas was resting in his chair, Thomas said, "Thanks, son. I should tell you something. You know already that I was a soldier before your mom passed away."

Henry replied, "Yes, Dad, I remember."

"That man you tried to help—Christian—I grew up with him. He used to live in a hut near here, but his parents were murdered there when he was a boy. He was taken in by King William and raised as his own. William sent him away to another country when an attempt on William's life was made. When Christian came back, he remembered me. He gave me an option to be a soldier, and I trained with him. When your mom got sick, he gave me an option. I could continue as a soldier or leave so I could stay here with you. I decided I should stay with you. He agreed with me that I should leave my post and take care of you." Thomas gasped a little due to the pain he was in.

"Dad, you should stop talking and lie down," Henry said.

Thomas replied, "Son, I need you to hear this. What you did was right. People here are afraid with good reason. People have been killed trying to help Christian. He is like family to me, and it hurts that I have not done anything to help him. You are my son and come first."

Henry said, "Dad, do you not always say we should take care of family?"

Thomas replied, "Son, you are right, but if I did what you did, I would be dead. Do not throw stones at soldiers. You might be killed! Do not do that again. You are a good son. Now get us something to eat while I sit here by the fire."

STRENGTH IS HERE

From his position in the woods, Cassian could hear a horn blow. The horn kept on calling him to move forward. Cassian soon found himself at the edge of the woods. He could see a man brought out to the huts outside of the castle walls. At first glance, Cassian thought he recognized who the man was. He did not look like Christian at all. The man was smaller, dirty, and seemed to be a shell of a man. The man walked with his head down and obeyed his masters, the soldiers. When the man looked up, Cassian was shocked to recognize Christian. Cassian watched as Christian was whipped. He wanted to help, but he knew there was nothing he could do. After the whipping, Cassian headed back into the woods. He found Alexander and described what he had seen. Cassian went into detail about how Christian acted, and the severity of the whipping. Cassian said, "I need to get this information to Curtis. We will see what our next steps are going to be."

Alexander said, "From what you say there doesn't seem to be much fight in him at all."

Cassian replied, "We don't know the whole situation. What I observed may not be the case for him. I will pass it on for them to get the message to him."

Alexander said, "I'll be fine. What you saw should come from you and no one else. You saw it."

"I see what you're saying," Cassian said. "I'll ask Bard to come down here and join you. Stay safe." They interlocked arms and nodded to each other. Cassian took off through the woods. When he got to the cliff, he yelled, "Bard! Are you there?" There was no response. Cassian called for him again. He could not see Bard, and Bard did not respond. Cassian yelled, "Are you sleeping up there?"

Bard answered, "I heard you the first time. Why are you coming up?"

"I need to get a message to Curtis about Christian. I'm going to need you to go with Alexander."

Bard paused because he did not want to leave his post.

"I know what Curtis said about this post, but I do need to see him," Cassian replied.

Bard threw a rope down to Cassian. When Cassian reached the top Bard looked over to his right. "Abel, you are on your own for a while. The horses are over there. Can you let me down?" Bard got himself ready, and Abel let him down the hill. Cassian got on a horse and headed toward the encampment.

***

Christian was brought back to his cell in the dungeon. One of the soldiers was smiling. "Ben, here is your patient for you to take care of. Get him better so we can do this again."

Ben saw Christian's back. There were so many healing scars already on his back, and now there were new open slashes into the skin. Ben addressed the soldiers. "How much more can you do? He has scars all over." Christian motioned to him to stop speaking.

Christian spoke softly, "My back may look bad, but it does not hurt me as much as it did when they whipped me before. I prayed to God before they started. The pain from the whip was bearable."

Ben replied, "Why does God not stop them from doing this?"

Christian paused. "I am sure God has a plan. I am still living. Only God knows what my fate should be. I will not question God.

It is a blessing to me that you are here to take care of me. I am going to lie down so you can tend to my back."

As Christian lay down, Ben thought to himself, *He called me a blessing God. If he only knew what I have done. Please forgive me, God, and help me take care of him.* Christian fell asleep as Ben took care of his back.

***

The next day, Cassian arrived at the encampment. It was not like the first time he had seen it. It appeared to be more of a military camp preparing for war. People were training with swords and bows while others were exercising or working. There was more structure as they were preparing for their survival. On the training fields, he found Curtis. Alec, Edmund, and Joseph noticed Cassian and walked to him. "I saw Christian the other day outside of the castle walls," Cassian said.

Curtis asked, "How did he look?" Cassian started talking as Elizabeth and Agatha arrived to bring equipment to Alec.

Cassian replied, "I didn't recognize him at first. He didn't walk with the pride he had before. He seemed to be more a shell of a man who was obeying his masters. He looked beaten. There was no fight in him."

Elizabeth, hearing what was said, stepped into the conversation. "Did he kneel right away after the first whipping?"

"No," replied Cassian.

Elizabeth seemed to become boulder. "How many times did they whip him?"

Cassian replied, "I lost count. The beating was very severe. He fell to his knee once but fought to pick himself up."

"Now, men, even I can see Christian has fight in him," she said. "I saw them beat him, and it was brutal. He would not fold. He did not ask for mercy. The first time it was done, people tried to rescue him, but they were killed. After that, he asked people not to intervene. He did not want them to lose their lives on account of him." Elizabeth then looked at Cassian, "Now you tell these men he has no fight in him. You have no right to say that to these men. He has more fight in him than any of you. We have been preparing for a war. Now, if you men are not going to do something to rescue him, let me know. I will get some women to help me." Agatha tried to pull Elizabeth away from the conversation, and she left reluctantly with brief parting words: "Let me know."

Curtis looked at the men and said, "Let's plan what we are going to do." They all agreed.

Alec said, "That tree line is our defense point. Get some men and women up in the trees. Have some on the ground. We will stop them if they charge us. Our people's skills have improved drastically."

Curtis said, "Let's get some horses down there ready to charge if needed be."

Cassian said, "We should have some people in the field who are good archers. I think Elizabeth was right about one thing for sure. We should allow the women to be there to attack the soldiers and free Christian."

Curtis said, "If necessary, I will take men to charge the walls to get to Christian."

Alec said, "We will have to come up with a solid plan. We have a time span of four to six weeks. It all depends on Brutus."

Curtis replied, "We should start getting some provisions in the woods." The men all agreed. Curtis and Edmund went off to plan on what they would need down there. Alec and Joseph continued training the townspeople.

***

After a few days had passed, Christian was starting to recover. He started to do some exercises that did not affect his back. Ben looked at what Christian was doing and said, "You should be taking it easy."

Christian looked at him and replied, "My back is fine. I need to get back in shape as much as I can. I am through taking it easy."

"I think you are overdoing it," Ben commented.

"I heard one of the soldiers comment that I am getting weak. He was right. I have done nothing."

"Don't tell me you are listening to the soldiers now."

"Something inside of me is telling me I need to get back in shape. I need to be ready."

"Do you think you are going to get out of here?"

"My faith tells me yes. I do not believe this is the end of me. I told you the whip did not hurt as much this last time." Christian paused, looked down, and then looked at Ben. "I look back at my life and I see there has always been something driving me forward. Something inside of me tells me to keep on going. My spirit screams inside of me to keep on fighting, to not give up. I must keep moving forward."

Ben asked, "What about sins that you have committed? Do they not put weight on you?"

Christian looked up and became quiet. "I have confessed my sins to God and repented. Still, at times, I do think about things I have done. I know God forgives, but I remember at times what I did, and I see how I hurt others. That is what hurts me. As for forgiveness, I am just a man, and God is much greater than I. If God can forgive me, I should be able to forgive myself and others. Jesus Christ died for our sins."

Ben seemed to find a little peace and decided to lie down. He soon fell asleep.

A few days passed, and a guard saw Christian exercising yet again. He informed Carl, who went to Christian's cell to see for himself what Christian was doing. "What are you doing, Christian? You are not trying to get some of your strength back, are you?" asked Carl.

Christian looked at him. "It is however you take it."

Carl reacted to this by calling the guards. "Put him in a different

cell. Cut his portion of food. We want to keep him manageable."
He turned back to Christian. "I do not need you to bulk back up."

***

A week passed, and at the encampment, the people continued
their training. Joseph sought out Luisa and took her to Curtis's
tent. When they arrived, they found Curtis, Alec, and Emma inside
talking. Curtis spoke up. "I had both of you women brought here
because we need your help to free Christian."

Luisa became a little nervous. "What would you have us do?"

Curtis said, "First, I need to know if you will help. I do not want
anyone who is not involved to know our plan. It will be dangerous."

Luisa looked at Joseph, and a sense of bravery overwhelmed her
"I know this man is important to you. For this reason, I will help.
Emma, will you do this with me?"

Emma responded, "Yes, but I want to know why us?"

Curtis smiled, glad they had agreed to help, "Emma you know
all the castle grounds. Both of you know how to use the bow and
are getting better with the sword. The main reason is that you are
young and able to run fast if something goes wrong. Also, no one
will expect women in the role of soldiers."

Luisa looked at Curtis and started to speak, but she turned to
Joseph and said, "What would you have us do?"

Curtis said, "We are going to have you two go live in a hut
outside of the castle in a few weeks. There is a place all ready for you
there. I want you two to know that we will be in the woods guarding
you. If something happens, we will come charging." Curtis looked
at them. "This is what we are going to have you do—when you hear
the horn blown, it will be time to start in action."

***

In two weeks, Curtis and his men managed to get horses in the
woods. They reviewed their plans and found hiding places for the

soldiers that were also good vantage points for their archery skills. They determined the range of their arrows and put up markers that only they would recognize. Most of this was done in the darkness so no one would see them. In the third week, Luisa and Emma got ready to move into the hut that had been prepared for them. Joseph found Luisa alone. "I Love you. You are strong, and you will be fine. If something happens, I will come, as so will others."

Luisa grabbed Joseph and kissed him. "I Love you too. I must go now." In the cover of darkness, Luisa and Emma made their way to the hut that was going to house them until Christian was once again publicly whipped.

***

A few weeks more passed at the castle grounds. One afternoon, Carl went to see Brutus. Brutus asked, "Any signs of Curtis and his men?"

Carl replied, "There has not been any sign of them, but I feel they are out there."

Brutus said, "They are out there, but I know there will come a time when they come. We should do something to provoke them."

Carl asked, "Why? Let them stay out there."

Brutus said, "The longer they wait, the stronger they will be. I am worried that they will be stronger than we expect when they come after us."

Carl replied, "I will take Christian out further from the castle next time so they can see him from the woods. I believe someone is watching from there. We have checked before but have not seen anyone."

Brutus said, "Take a few extra soldiers with you. I'm going to stay here." Carl nodded and headed to the dungeon with a contingent of soldiers.

"Christian! Christian!" Carl called for him. "It's that time again, Christian." Christian came forward. "You do not look so good.

You look like you lost a lot of weight. I guess it's because we are not feeding you as well as we did before." Carl paused. "After today that might change." He turned to the guards and said, "Put restraints on Christian so we can take him out of the dungeon."

Christian looked at them. "Ten of you to take me out? Are you worried I might be freed?"

Carl replied, "Not so worried about that. No one has bothered to rescue you yet. They know what will happen." Once they got outside, one of the soldiers blew the horn to let people know what was going on. People cleared the area; they did not want any part of Christian's torture. They were afraid for their own lives.

Emma and Luisa heard the horn and headed toward the sound. Henry heard the horn and walked toward the sound.

The soldiers took Christian to the edge of the field to an old fencepost that had only the top rail—a crosspiece—left. While the soldiers checked out the post, Thomas arrived at his hut to see if Henry was still there, but he noticed that Henry had left. Thomas grabbed his sword and threw it in the front of his wagon. He headed toward the sound of the horn.

After the soldiers finished checking the fencepost, one soldier observed, "The fence will be strong enough to hold Christian. That is as long as he does not struggle."

Carl said, "Attach him to it then."

Christian looked up from the fencepost, and he saw the field where his hut used to be. He started to be saddened.

Emma and Luisa kept their distance because of the number of soldiers that were around Christian. Two guards each took one of his arms and tied it to the fencepost. Out of nowhere, Henry came running up tried to hinder them from securing Christian's arms. One of the soldiers threw Henry to the ground and said, "Stay there, little boy." Henry got up and again tried to hinder them.

Christian noticed what was happening and asked God to give him strength. He started to feel stronger, and he moved his head and ducked underneath the fencepost, resting the crosspiece across his shoulders. Christian pushed upward with his legs and was able to pull the post from the ground; it was still chained to his body. He put the fencepost in front of him and started to fight the soldiers. Some of the soldiers were trying to secure Christian while others were laughing. Christian yelled, "Leave the little boy be!" Thomas arrived and jumped from his wagon, sword in hand. One soldier fell instantly to Thomas sword. Thomas yelled, "Henry, get on the wagon and control the horses." Thomas took down another soldier as ran at him. An arrow struck down one more soldier, and then another arrow found its target.

Emma and Luisa constantly fired arrows at the soldiers, killing a few more. One arrow hit Carl in his shoulder, and he took off running at the gate yelling for more soldiers. Christian continued to fight. Thomas moved toward Christian and helped him kill another soldier. As he was fighting one more soldier, Thomas yelled to Christian, "Get on the wagon!" Christian struggled to get on the wagon.

As Emma and Luisa ran toward the wagon, Luisa gave Emma her bow, drew her sword, and faced a soldier who was charging them. The soldier swung as if to take off Luisa's head, but she ducked and stabbed him in his side in one flowing motion. The soldier fell to the ground. Finally, Emma and Luisa arrived at the wagon. They unwrapped the metal chains from around the wooden post and helped get Christian in the wagon. Thomas finished off the last soldier and yelled to Henry, "Take us to the woods as fast as you can. We cannot fight them on open ground." Henry whipped up the horses, and the wagon headed for the woods.

Luisa yelled as she pointed ahead, "Head in that direction. We have people waiting." They continued to watch the castle gate to see if anyone came out. In less than a minute, they looked back at the castle gates and saw soldiers coming after them on horseback. Henry was driving the wagon as fast as he could, but the soldiers were gaining on them. Emma and Luisa took positions so they could shoot the few arrows they had left.

At the edge of the woods, Curtis, Alec, and the others watched what was going on. Curtis hopped onto his horse and said, "Let's charge!"

Alec grabbed Curtis's horse reins and said, "Not yet!"

Curtis replied, "They need us!"

"I am not going to sacrifice anyone's life today. They will make it, and you will see arrows fly." Curtis got off his horse and got into position to shoot arrows.

Henry drove the horses as fast as he could, but the soldiers started to gain on the wagon. Emma and Luisa continued to shoot at the soldiers in front. Emma killed one, and he fell, but the others kept coming. Soon they were three hundred feet from the woods. Alec saw the wagon go past one of the markers and yelled, "Two hundred fifty feet!" The newly trained fighters let their arrows fly. A few of Brutus's soldiers fell to the ground. Other soldiers continued to charge at them. Alec yelled, "Two hundred feet!" The archers shot more arrows. More soldiers fell to the ground, but the survivors kept on charging at the wagon. Soon the remaining soldiers were within one hundred fifty feet. Alec yelled, "Let the arrows fly!"

Soon all of Brutus's soldiers fell to the ground, dead or dying. Around twenty more soldiers had lost their lives. When the wagon finally made it to the woods, Curtis's men ran forward, rejoicing that they had saved Christian. Thomas and Henry got off the wagon and embraced each other. Curtis, however, could not recognize Christian. Christian was not responsive to them, but they could see he was breathing.

Luisa ran to Joseph. Joseph said, "I am so proud of you! I'm glad you are safe."

In desperation, Curtis yelled, "Joseph, we need a stretcher to carry Christian to safety!" They hurried to get one together. Curtis turned toward his people. "Does anyone have a key for the shackles?" Alec gave him one, saying, "I figured we would need one." Curtis smiled and removed the remaining chains from Christian. The men put Christian on the stretcher and moved as quickly as they could to the cliff. Another wave of Brutus's soldiers charged into the woods. Half of them fell to arrows. The remaining soldiers soon retreated.

***

During the battle, a messenger returned to the castle to tell Brutus what was going on. He ran toward the castle gates. More soldiers were getting ready to ride out, but Brutus stopped them. "Where is Carl?" he demanded.

A soldier replied, "He went to get an arrow removed from his shoulder."

Brutus said, "When the remaining soldiers come back, close this gate. We will now prepare for them to come after us." Brutus started to walk away, but he stopped. "Find Carl and have him report to me." A soldier left to get Carl for Brutus. A few hours later, Carl reported to Brutus. Brutus asked, "How is your shoulder?"

"The arrow was not too deep."

"Why are you alive while everyone else is dead?" Carl became very silent and did not respond. Brutus said, "I think we know the answer. This is what you are going to do for me. Find your nephew, for I have a mission for him. Also, find that gate guard who survived, Charles, and Bertram whom I sent out to find Curtis and his men. Bring them to me for I have a mission for them."

***

Back in the woods, the troops reached the cliff and hooked up a harness to lift Christian up. Curtis headed up the cliff first to help with Christian. While they were bringing him up, Bard said, "Is he dead? I don't see any movement."

Curtis replied, "He is still breathing. You are not going to recognize him. Who knows what he went through while in captivity, but I do believe he will recover. I do believe God has a purpose for him."

Bard got a good look at Christian. "He does not look much like himself."

Curtis replied, "He was able to defend Thomas's boy, Henry, from the soldiers with a fencepost before others came to his aid."

They got Christian up to the top of the cliff and removed the harness. They picked him up and carried him to a wagon they had ready. As soon as Emma and Luisa both were brought up the cliff, they got into the wagon to help with Christian. Curtis got the horses going on their trek back to the encampment. During this time, Christian remained unresponsive.

They get back to the encampment in the middle of the night. Curtis picked Christian up and carried him into a tent where they had prepared a bed for him. They decided to first clean his wounds for they were worried they might become infected.

One of the night watchers had gone to tell Edmund they had arrived, and he soon arrived at the tent where they were tending Christian. Edmund entered the tent and said, "How is he?" Edmund walked forward, and he, too, barely recognized Christian.

Curtis replied, "He does not look like himself at all. Looks like they barely fed him. This might have been his last day if we had not rescued him. The good thing is that we did not lose anyone on our side. If he recovers, that is one thing he will ask. Around thirty of Brutus's soldiers did lose their lives today."

Emma and Luisa rolled Christian onto his side, and they saw all of scars on his back. They could find no words to say; they were truly saddened. The women finished cleaning and bandaging his back and laid him back down and covered him with a warm blanket. Luisa said, "I will stay with him tonight in case he wakes."

Curtis responded, "I will stand guard tonight as well."

Edmund said, "In the morning, we will discuss what we are going to do. Right now, it seems he needs his sleep."

TIME TO GET
READY

I n the middle of the night, a twelve-year-old boy showed up in the woods and was met by Cassian. Three soldiers left the castle on horseback. The boy told Cassian that he had lost his father because they thought he was involved in helping rescue Christian. Cassian believed him and took care of him until others were ready to go back to the encampment.

***

In the morning, Carl found Brutus and said, "What you asked was done last night."

Brutus replied, "I do not think either plan will work, but I must try one last time. I am not going to send out more soldiers after them. It seems they have been more successful in open battle. I know Christian will come, and that is when we need to be ready. I do not want to push our men too much, for I do not know how many are truly loyal to us. We have lost many that were, and some of these new recruits we have I feel would rather attack us. Make sure they do not abuse the townspeople, for they now might be emboldened to attack us." Carl departed from Brutus.

***

At the encampment, Christian was still asleep. Curtis and Edmund discussed what they should do to keep him safe. Elizabeth, Emma, Luisa, and Agatha rotated keeping watch over Christian as men were posted outside.

A few days passed, and Christian was still unresponsive; he was barely breathing. The townspeople were starting to worry.

At the cliff, nothing else happened so Alec, the little boy, and others decided to head back to the encampment. They arrived in the evening. He was met by his oldest son, William, who ran to him. "Dad, I see you brought Richard back with you."

Alec looked confused, "Who?"

William responded, "Richard. He is Carl's nephew. Richard talks about him all the time." Alec told the other men who were with him, and they ran to find Richard. They did not see him, so they ran to the tents and found two soldiers standing in the doorway. One of them was Curtis, and he saw Alec running toward the tent. Alec yelled to him, "A boy might be in there to kill Christian!" Curtis let him go by and entered the tent. They found Richard in there with a knife in his hand. Alec drew his sword and said, "Richard, let me have the knife. I know you were sent here, but at your age, you should not be ordered to kill a man. Do not start this type of life. There is so much more." Richard slowly walked toward Alec as if to strike him.

Curtis drew his sword. "Drop that knife or I will cut off your head!" Richard dropped the knife. Curtis glared at Richard and said, "It was a good idea for me to stand at the opposite tent. I never thought they would turn a child into a killer."

Alec dragged Richard out of the tent and away from the area. People were talking loudly because of what Richard had been ordered to do. This attracted Elizabeth's attention. She had been watching Christian, but she left the tent.

Something had happened to awaken Christian. He looked outside the tent and saw a boy sitting on a log looking at him. The boy was weeping quietly. The fabric over the tent door kept blowing open and shut in the breeze, blocking Christian's steady view of the boy. Christian managed to get up. He struggled to get through the tent door. When he got outside, he did not see the boy. He asked Curtis, "Where is the little boy who was sitting on that log?"

Curtis said, "There was no boy out here sitting on a log." Christian started to fall, but Elizabeth caught him. One of Edmund's original people, Col, saw what was happening. Col started laughing at Christian and said sarcastically, "This is your leader?" Curtis became offended and punched Col, knocking him to the ground.

Christian saw this and stood up as tall as he could and walked closer to Curtis, "You should not be doing that." Christian spun around fast and hit Curtis in the face with his elbow. This made them both unsteady on their feet.

Curtis smiled. "Now that is what I want to see. I can see they have not broken you, Christian."

"They have not broken me. I will fight for our people to be free."

"I will follow you when that day comes, but right now you have to get your strength back."

"Did you lose anyone trying to rescue me?"

"We did not lose anyone, but thirty more of Brutus's men fell."

"I heard about what you did to Brutus's soldiers. He got a little upset and took it out on me. The scars on my back may be many, but I am fine. I am worried about our people."

"Let's get you fed, and we can discuss a plan. I want Alec to be involved."

Christian looked puzzled. "Alec?"

Curtis replied, "I know he trained Brutus's soldiers, but he helped plan your escape and kept me from charging twice into battle when I did not need to." Christian looked at him. Curtis said, "Brutus sent Carl's nephew here to kill you. Alec helped me stop him." Curtis got Christian back in his tent so he could rest. "I will get you some food," he said. "And I'll bring Alec."

***

Three days later, the three soldiers sent out by Brutus arrived near the campsite where Bertram's comrades had been killed. Bertram pointed. "Over that mound is the ravine where we were staying." They started to move forward, and Charles noticed a piece of a soldier's garment hanging off a tree branch. Charles was fixated on that scrap of cloth. "Stop! I'm going to see why this cloth is here." Charles saw that a branch was broken. He figured it was a path marker. He said, "Come this way. It seems one of the other soldiers was following someone." Bertram and the other soldiers rode over to Charles. Charles said, "Look at this path that was marked. It appears the soldier went east. I think we should ride that way."

Bertram replied, "I think we should head back and inform Brutus."

Charles said, "I think we need to make sure first, just in case Brutus does want to attack them." They headed east through the brush heading until they came to open land. Charles said, "Keep heading east for now. Let's be cautious." They continued to move forward until they made it to the river where they found a dead body lying in the open. Charles examined it. "It appears we found one of those soldiers. They did not even bother to hide the body. They must want to be found or are leaving a message. Let's camp here tonight."

Bertram replied, "It is only midday, and why would you want to camp here?"

Charles said, "The horses need water and so do we. I don't see anyone around us. I want to be well rested, and we can leave early in the morning. If it bothers you, you can go on." The soldiers gathered wood and took care of the horses. They waited till night fell to start a fire. As they were settling in, Charles said, "I wonder about what has been going on. Are we following the right man?"

Bertram started to get angry, "He is your king, and you will honor him."

Charles said, "The only reason I say this is because one will have you killed for his own power while the other will give up his life and not want you to sacrifice yours. That is all I mean."

Bertram yelled, "You are talking treason!"

Charles shook his head, "Maybe I don't know what I am talking about. It has been a long ride, and I am going to take a nap. We can take shifts through the night." Charles lay down and closed his eyes. He was soon asleep. Bertram unsheathed his sword and walked toward Charles. The soldier, who had not given them his name, was sitting next to Charles. The unnamed soldier kicked him to wake him up. Charles opened his eyes and found the unnamed soldier and Bertram facing each other, swords drawn. Charles stood, drew his sword as well, and said, "What is going on?"

The unnamed soldier replied, "Bertram was going to kill you in your sleep."

Bertram said, "Charles, you deserve to die. You probably did help Alec leave."

Charles said to the unnamed soldier, "If that is true, then put your sword back and step away. This is between Bertram and me." The unnamed soldier backed away and put his sword away. Charles faced Bertram with his sword held at the ready. "Let us finish this then. You are right, I did help Alec and his family escape. The other soldier raped my fiancé, and he knew about my engagement. He did it because he was allowed to and wanted to." Bertram charged at Charles, swinging his sword. Charles was able to stop Bertram's blade from hitting him. The clanging of blades went on. Charles could see Bertram was getting tired. Finally, he was able to strike Bertram's right hand. This made Bertram lose his grip on his sword. Charles struck Bertram's sword, knocking it out of his hand. He stabbed Bertram, killing him instantly. Charles looked at the unnamed soldier and put his sword away, "Thanks. Why did you save me?"

The unnamed soldier replied, "That man was a coward, and I would not show any allegiance to him. I figure you should be alerted to fight for your life and not have it stolen from you."

"Thanks again. I figure that, at dawn, we will try to find them." Charles stepped back a little. "I will confess I am going to join them. My fiancé is with them now. It is true what I said about Christian.

Life was better before he was put in chains." The unnamed soldier nodded. Charles asked, "Why have you not given us your name?"

The unnamed soldier replied, "I have my reasons, and I will support us finding this encampment." He paused. "Do not worry. I do not wish harm against them. I to plan to join them too." The unnamed soldier looked again at Charles. "Listen, I will go to sleep first and let you take first watch. If I am still alive and I am able to wake up, I will believe we can trust each other. From the events that happened earlier, you must realize that I want you to live." The unnamed soldier fell asleep while Charles stayed on watch.

At dawn, Charles and the unnamed soldier got ready. "So, you let me sleep all night. Did you fall asleep?" asked the unnamed soldier.

Charles replied, "I stayed awake. I know you saved my life, and I am going to have you come with me."

The unnamed soldier said, "I am glad for that. So, are you ready to go?"

Charles replied, "Yes. Let me tie this white piece of fabric to my sword. I am going to display it. Let us move slowly. I do not want them to think we are charging them." The two men continued to head east. In a few hours, they saw a long wall. Charles stopped. "I think we have found what we are looking for."

The unnamed soldier replied, "I do agree with you. Lift your sword so they can see your white flag."

Charles said, "Let's move slowly now and not make any fast movements." They got closer and closer to the wall.

The unnamed soldier said, "I see movement up there."

Charles looked around. "It seems they are trying to get around us. Someone should come to us shortly. Let me speak for us." Soon they were surrounded by soldiers, Joshua among them.

Joshua said, "I see your white flag. What do you want here?"

Charles replied, "My name is Charles. I am the soldier who helped Alec escape that night. Also, my fiancée is here. Her name is Emma."

Joshua looked at the unnamed soldier. "What about him?"

The unnamed soldier replied, "I have come to join you as well."

Joshua said, "What is your name?"

The soldier replied, "I will share that when I feel the time is right."

Joshua spoke in a deeper voice. "I feel the time is right now."

The unnamed soldier replied, "I might be very beneficial to your cause, but I will withhold my name for a while longer."

Joshua started to show rage, "Tell me your name now or—"

Charles interrupted him. "I will vouch for this soldier. He saved my life."

Joshua said, "Let me have his sword then."

The unnamed soldier replied, "You are making it tough for me, but if I must, here it is." He unbuckled his sword slowly and gave it to Joshua.

Joshua calmed down some. "Let's head to the camp and find Alec. Crispin, can you make sure they were not followed?"

Charles replied, "We are the only ones. Brutus realized he is losing soldiers in open ground. I do not think he will be sending anyone else out to find you. He decided to try one last time with us."

Crispin said, "I will go check and head back to the wall."

Joseph turned his horse. "Let us go now." They learned that Alec was with Christian, so they rode to Christian's tent. As they got off their horses, the unnamed soldier grabbed a big sack from the back of his horse. Joshua went into the tent first with his sword. He ushered Charles in while the unnamed soldier stayed in the doorway. Joshua pointed to the unnamed soldier. "Alec, do you know this man?"

Alec stepped forward and smiled. "This is the soldier who helped save my life. I trust him."

Joshua motioned for the unnamed soldier to enter the tent. "We have another soldier that was with him. He did not want to tell us his name. It started to get into an argument." The soldier entered carrying the big sack, and Christian lock eyes with him, "David!" The men in the tent started to get tense.

David replied, "I see you remember me. You do not look so good. I hope I did not make the wrong decision."

Christian said, "Last time I saw you, you were at King Archibald's side doing his dirty work."

David replied in a cocky manner, "I think we can say the same for you. You and I know the people you talked to usually ended up dead. I did not have to kill, but I could have if I had to."

Christian said, "Why have you come here?"

David took a step forward, "First, I have a gift for you that I took from Brutus." David opened the sack, unrolled a blanket, and spilled out swords, knives, and a shield with straps. Christian's eyes opened and his posture became emboldened. He sat up taller. Others in the tent started to smile. The items were Christian's battle gear. David said, "I am glad to see you like this. Now tell me, did I make the right choice to join you? Like you, I lost favor with King Archibald, and that is why I am here with you."

David picked up Christian's sword. It was still in its scabbard. He turned the handle toward Christian. Alec took out his sword as well. David walked toward Christian and said again, "Did I make the right choice, Christian? Or is it Hope? The people's Hope." David put Christian's sword closer to Christian, and Christian grasped the sword's handle. David walked back, removing the scabbard from Christian's sword. Christian held his sword in his hand. He stood up and started to swing his sword a little. His entire demeanor changed. He felt strength come back to him. He felt stronger than ever before. His confidence increased as did the confidence of all who witnessed this exchange. Hope seemed to come back to the people in the tent. David stepped back and said, "I am thinking I made the right choice."

Christian replied, "David, you are free to stay here, but I do not know how much I trust you yet." His voice changed; it became deeper more commanding as he said, "Joshua, I am glad you did not get in a sword fight with David. I have seen him in action with a sword. You would have lost. He could have taken us all once he had my sword in his hand."

David replied, "I think now I am second to you. I see you have that fire in your eyes like you used to have, especially when you were a gladiator."

Edmund walked into the tent and saw David. They locked eyes, and David said, "I am liking my choice even better now that I see you, Edmund. Look at Christian and tell me what you see." Edmund looked at Christian. He remembered how Christian looked when he was in the arena. "Is that not the look he had that made you stop being a gladiator? You knew at some point you would have to fight him. You chose life instead of going for fame," said David.

Edmund replied, "I do remember."

Christian said, "David, that is enough. As I said, you may walk freely, but I want you escorted. If I were a cautious man, I would have you put in a cage, but I know choices a person makes to stay alive and to keep others safe."

David was about to speak, but Christian put up his hand and said, "In fact, David, if you really want to help, I want you to help Alec teach our people sword fighting. For right now, I want you to use a wooden sword. No disrespect, but I know how lethal you can be."

David responded, "I can do that."

Christian spoke to Alec and Edmund. "Can you get David some food and then take him to the training field?" He turned to Charles. "Emma is out there. She helped rescue me. I hope you two can figure something out." Charles, David, Alec, and Edmund then left the tent.

Christian said, "Joshua can you get me a couple buckets of water?" After Joshua left, Christian looked at his sword and got on his knees and prayed. "Thank you, God. When you woke me up from my sleep, I saw a child. It was a child who brought back my faith and my love for you. You were with me when I was in the dungeon, and you had me rescued. Now I have my sword. With your guidance, I will free my people—your people. I am my father's son, and I will see that you are the only God that is honored by my

Hope Is it on Time

people. For I know everything is yours, and I am just a steward of what belongs to you. I love you, God, Jesus, and the Holy Spirit. Amen."

Joseph soon returned with the water. Christian poured the water over his sword, knives, and shield. Joseph said, "So you do not trust David?"

Christian responded, "I never really got to know him, but I know who he was with most of the time. It appears there is nothing wrong with my equipment. Take the blanket and burn it to be safe. Only touch the dry part." Joseph left with the blanket.

Christian started to maneuver with his sword. He remembered how awkward he had been when he first started training. He felt the same now, but the more he moved, the more he improved. He felt his body remembering moves that he used to make without thinking. Christian's moves become more fluid, and he was dancing! He first moved slowly and found accuracy in the strikes he made. He worked up speed using all the force he had in his strikes. He noticed that his endurance and agility were lacking. He sat down and put his head down. He looked at his sword in a trance, focusing on it. He started to think about his past life and the experiences he had gone through, but he stopped and became grateful. He humbled himself to God and thought about his people who were under Brutus's control. The fire inside him ignited, and he took up his sword once more and started moving around the tent as if he was fighting actual enemies. Every motion was fluid. He looked down at the floor and saw his two identical long knives. He sheathed his long sword and picked up the knives, one in each hand. As he examined them, he remembered what he could do with them. He got into a defensive stance, held up the knives, and struck the air with one while using the other to block an imaginary attack. He moved around in the tent, dancing with his knives, striking objects that were not there. The more he did it, the more fluid his moves became. He stopped finally and smiled as he looked at all his battle equipment. He strapped the shield to his back and slipped on

107

the sheaths that held his two knives. Then he strapped his sword around his waist, left the tent, and started to run.

***

After they ate a small meal, Alec and Edmund took David to a field where some of the people were training with swords. David watched and said sarcastically, "Oh, that looks nice. Can I have a sword so I can see their skill?"

Joshua said, "There is a wooden sword over there."

"Oh, that's right. You do not trust me with a blade. Okay." David joined the trainees and grabbed the wooden sword. The people stopped what they had been doing, and David looked around at them. "Which among you is the best?" he asked.

They looked around, and one man came forward and said, "I would say I am."

David replied, "I want to spar with you. You can keep that metal sword. Let me see what you can do." The man hesitated. David said, "Trust me. I will be fine." The man swung repeatedly at David, but he blocked all the blows because he knew exactly what the man was going to do. David said, "That is nice, but can you do more?" The man, obviously frustrated, swung even harder. David noticed that the man was getting tired, so he started to taunt him by striking his back and his legs. He slapped the wooden sword across the man's butt. The man got red and charged at David. In one motion, David hit the man's hand and took away his sword. The man stepped forward, facing David. David picked up the metal blade and held it in front of the man, and the man backed off. David looked at Edmund and Alec and said, "Their basic swings are good, but I could tell he could not do that forever. There are more moves to learn, and his endurance is lacking." David threw down the metal sword. He then looked past Edmund and Alec and said, "Look over there. That man knows what he must do to be number one." Alec and Edmund looked behind them and saw Christian running in full gear. Others in the encampment had heard that Christian was there, but they had not seen him until now.

Alec said, "All right, men, strap up. Let's do more physical training than we have been doing." Alec looked at Edmund and then at David and said, "David, will you help us train our people?"

David looked around, "Sure! I have nothing else better to do right now."

A few weeks passed, and Christian felt that his original strength and stamina had returned even though his body was still recovering. He was starting to look as he used to. During this time, he helped train the people. People were starting to be more confident in their capabilities as well. They did not have the fear they had before of being invaded or of soldiers taking advantage of them.

***

At the castle, Brutus had made a few changes, but he was also a little anxious. He made his rounds in the castle grounds and ran into Carl. Brutus said, "My last two plans have failed." Carl stared at Brutus, and Brutus said, "Knock it off. I'm sure your nephew is alive. Christian is not like us. He will not have him put to death. I'm sure they will be coming for us any time, and I'm sure Christian is fully recovered. I had his sword, knives, and shield, but they are now missing. I am sure he has them."

Carl said, "How do you think he will attack?"

Brutus said, "I do not think we will see him coming, but at some point, he is going to have to breach this gate. That is our only defense. He might have other plans of attack. All our soldiers might not support us. Our most loyal ones have lost their lives already."

Carl replied, "It seems that you have convinced yourself we are going to lose."

Brutus took a deep breath. "The only way to stop them is to take out Christian, but if I know Curtis and others who are left, I am sure they have all been training and will be a force we will have to deal with."

***

Back at the encampment, Christian was out training with his sword and knives when Col approached him. Col shook his head and said, "Why are you going back to the castle? We have it good here, don't we?"

Christian replied, "Those who are at the castle are my people."

Col said, "Are we not your people as well?"

Christian replied, "Yes, the people here are my people as well, and I will fight for them. The people at the castle are my people too. They have done nothing wrong to be in the situation they are in. Let me say this: If someone came and took you from us against your will, I would go after you just as I must go to them." Col did not have anything to say. Christian said, "Col, I have seen how some of these people treat you. You do not disrespect them even though they disrespect you. You stay humble. I know there is strength in you. You will use it when you need to." Christian looked at Col. "God has a plan for you. I believe he has a purpose for each one of us. I believe he is using me to free my people and bring them back to him."

Col replied, "Do you not think that is too much?"

Christian said, "My father told me that a monastery once flourished in my kingdom. It was devoted to God. The people discovered gold in their stone quarry. A few of the monks sought their own desires. A king found out and wanted some of the gold. The monks denied the king his full share. The king just came and took it all. He appointed a mock king who would be loyal, and this king was ruthless to the people." Christian took a breath and looked at Col. "Look at where we are now. I have the people and a plan to save us. I do not think that happened by chance; it happened because of God." Col pondered what Christian had said, and he asked Christian if they could train together.

THE TIME
HAS COME

In the morning, Christian called for Edmund, Curtis, Joseph, and Alec to meet in his tent. Christian looked at them and said, "Do you men feel we are ready to take back the castle?"

Alec stepped forward. "Over these past weeks, our men have improved their fighting skills thanks to David's help. I feel they are ready." Joseph and Edmund nodded in agreement.

Curtis said, "Yeah, it is about time. Am I going to be able to charge?"

Christian replied, "Once the gates are open, you will be able to charge in." Curtis stood up a little taller. Christian said, "There is a tunnel that goes under the castle walls. It was used by the monks who were there before King Archibald took over. When the builders were building the castle walls, my dad braced the tunnel so it would not cave in. That part of the tunnel is solid rock. My dad took me there to check the braces. Before Brutus took over, I found the exterior entrance and followed the tunnel into the castle grounds. I did not want to destroy the wall to find out where it comes out."

Edmund asked, "What is your plan?"

"I had the blacksmith make a few bars we can use to pry any number of obstacles. I am going to have Edmund, Crispin, Joseph, Cassian, Col, Alec, and a few others come with me. When we enter the castle grounds, we will kill any of Brutus's soldiers who are there. A few men and I will exit the castle and go the main barracks where Brutus's most loyal soldiers stay. The rest will open the gates. They will be expecting some sort of attack, but they will be expecting it to come from the outside. Once the gates are open, Curtis, you will have only a little bit of time to get in. Other soldiers might charge the gates then."

Joseph said, "Why not take a lot of men inside the tunnel?"

Christian ignored Joseph for he did not want to put more men in danger. "The men who open the gates are going to be dressed as Luisa was. I want them to get as close to the gates as they can. I want all the attention to come to me so they have a better chance of opening the gates without being hurt. Alec and Edmund, I would like you to be with me." Alec and Edmund both accepted this.

Alec asked, "What about David?"

Christian replied, "I do not fully trust him."

Alec said, "I know you are good with a sword, but having another by your side would be beneficial." Alec paused, "What is your plan for Edmund and me?"

"I am going to take Col and both of you with your bows ready to take anyone down. As for David, go get him." Alec left.

In about fifteen minutes, he returned with David. David stepped in and looked around. He said, "This must be an important meeting. You are ready to attack them and have come up with a plan. So, tell me, are we going to charge the castle walls?" David looked at Christian. "No, I do not think so. You are more cunning than that and would not risk your men's lives that way. What is the plan then?"

Christian replied, "You will be filled in on the plan as it is happening. Alec and Edmund feel I need someone else who is good with a sword by my side. Can I trust you? Will you do that?"

David looked around and started removing something from his clothes as he said, "Well, I guess I no longer need to keep this knife I have hidden. I got it from someone here." David took the blade out

"The people here have treated me with more respect and kindness than anyone else ever has. I will do this with you. What will you have of me afterwards?"

Christian replied, "You are a free man and can do whatever you want just as long as you do not take advantage of anyone or hurt anyone. If you do not want to help us, that is also your choice."

David looked at Christian, "A free man. I can do that." Christian picked up a sword that he had standing in the corner and presented it to David. David accepted it while Christian took a few steps back. David looked at it and noticed it had changed a little. The handle and blade were engraved. He tested the balance and noticed that the blade had been sharpened. "Yes," he said to Christian, "I remember you also were trained by a blacksmith. This looks nice. No one has ever done such a thing for me. Especially no one who could be a king. I know this whole thing is not about getting you into a position of power. It is really to help your people and give them a better life. I will help you. So, when are we getting started?"

Christian turned to Curtis. "How many horses do we have at the bottom of the cliff?"

"We have three dozen." Christian was quiet. Curtis then said, "We have two options. I can send more now, and they will be there in a few days if they ride straight through or the rest run. It is not that far of a run, and I will be able to hold that gates open with thirty-six men."

Christian then said, "I will bring more with me. Get the people ready now. I want the best to come with us. Make sure we have people left here to protect the ones who cannot join us. I want to leave for the cliff in a few hours."

Alec asked, "Are we going to need provisions?"

Christian said, "What I have planned—if it goes right—will be done in a few hours. Bring only enough for three days. If that is not enough, we will send runners back to get what we need."

In a few hours, they left for the cliff. They did not have a lot of horses, so most were walking. Just before dusk, they stopped and made a camp. Christian asked Curtis, "How far are we from the cliff's edge?"

"It's about six hours if we keep the pace we did coming here."

Christian replied, "That is good then. I don't fully trust David. When we get to the bottom of the cliff, I don't want David to go to the wood's edge until it's time for us to move forward." Curtis looked at Christian and nodded. "I'm going to get a few more of our guys to keep watch then. We will take turns."

At dawn, everyone was ready to move again. In six hours, they arrived at the top of the cliff. Christian called for Alec to join him. They both went down a rope to the base of the cliff and then moved forward to the edge of the woods. Right before they got there, they were met by Cassian and Alexander. They all greet each other.

Cassian said, "I am glad to see you here. This can only mean that we will be taking back our castle."

Christian replied, "You are right. Let's go to the edge of the woods. I want you to tell me what their routine is." They moved forward through the woods and soon reached the edge. They observed what they could, taking every guard and movement at the castle walls into account.

Cassian said, "Ever since your rescue, they have put more people on the walls. I have not seen any soldiers go past that gate. They rely on only a few villagers to bring them food and supplies. I was told that a lot of the soldiers at the perimeter are forced to be there. The ones loyal to Brutus stay in the barracks at night."

Christian pondered a little. "I am going to change my plan. We will leave at nightfall. Cassian, I want you to go now and get the rest of your group—Edmund, Col, Thomas, and Alec." Curtis looked toward the castle walls.

Fifteen minutes later, Cassian arrived with the men Christian had asked for. David had decided to come of his own accord. Christian turned to them and said, "Men, the plan has changed. I see that you are here too, David."

David replied, "If I am going to risk my life, I want to know what's going on."

Christian continued, "Cassian informed me that most of the night guards are new soldiers who have been forced to guard the castle walls. I am going to bring fifty people with me through the tunnel. It will take us straight to the dungeon where there is a false wall. I didn't want to be specific about that before." He indicated some metal rods lying on the ground. "I have had these metal bars made. We can use them to force our way through the false wall. Joseph and Alec, I want you to lead a team to the gate. Curtis, you will stay here and lead the men in on foot. No horses. We need to do this silently and go around those huts. Do not take the shortest distance. Something does not seem right. Joseph, when you notice that castle wall guards have been removed, open the gates and signal Curtis with fire. Post people on the gates and keep your eyes open. Once everyone is inside the gates, secure them. After this is done, do not stand by it, but watch it. David, Edmund, Thomas, Cassian, Col, and ten others will come with me to take care of the soldiers who are in the two barracks. Alexander, I want you to take nine men with you and take out the soldiers who are roaming the streets. The rest of you, take some of those men and get behind the other castle wall guards. I want you guys to shoot an arrow at them to warn them. If someone raises a sword, bow, or sounds an alarm, shoot him. Replace the castle wall guard with one of our own. When you are getting into position, you might come across castle soldiers. You may have to kill them. I do not want anyone alerted. Thomas and Cassian, take a few men and go behind the barracks. Block the door and start a fire. Stay there and make sure no one comes out. If they do, take care of them. David, Edmund, and Col you will be with me at the other entrance with ten others. Once they start running out, we will use arrows until a few of us need to use our swords. Once we take care of the barracks and Curtis arrives with the men, we will head to the castle. At the castle, we need to watch the balcony for arrows coming upon us. I'm sure Brutus has soldiers in the castle.

Silence is our best ally in reaching our goals. Once the fire starts, it will attract everyone's attention. When you have taken care of your assignment, follow the wall back up to the castle gate and stay close to the buildings. Do not mass in one spot; keep moving forward. If you do capture soldiers, find a way to secure them so they are out of this until it is done. Are there any questions?"

David stepped forward and said, "Are you trying to keep an eye on me?" Some of the men looked at him questioningly.

Christian replied, "Yes. I also figure you would like to see the most action. Once they come out of those barracks, it will be nonstop fighting until they are all dead. So, you see, I am using your full potential."

David said, "I can handle that."

Christian replied, "At nightfall, we will make our way to the tunnel. I do not want people who are large in stature because the tunnel is tight for the first three hundred feet. Make sure all torches and lanterns remain unlit until we are twenty feet in. Cassian and Crispin, stand by the entrance and make sure of this. I will lead the way. Edmund and Col, you will be right behind me. So, find the people to come with us. Make sure no one is wearing armor. Now go and get some rest." The men left except for David and Curtis.

David said, "You sure your plan will work?"

Christian replied, "It must work. I will fight for my people."

David said, "Do you think everything is going to be done then? You know he will come."

Christian turned to look at the castle. Then he turned and looked at David. David looked into Christian's eyes, paused, and said, "You know this. You have a plan. Your plan involves the castle and its grounds. You are not worried about the numbers coming. No, I see in your eyes there is no worry. I am sure you know exactly what to do to save your people."

Christian said, "Go get some rest."

David smiled, "I am going to have to see this." Curtis and David then left Christian. Christian looked at the castle walls. He thought to himself, *Dad, I hope my plan will work to free our people. God, I will need you every step of the way. I pray that you will let me save my people. I Love you, God.*

As soon as night fell, they gathered together. Christian addressed his people: "Tonight we are going to save our people and take back our castle. Thank you for your help. I want to lead us in a prayer. God, I ask you to be with us and help us. Please keep us safe and guide us in taking over the castle. For I know everything is yours, God. Amen. Now let's go to the edge of the woods where the gully is. We need to follow that down for a while."

They started walking, following Christian down the gully about four hundred feet. They no longer could see the castle walls because the gully was so deep. Christian walked past a large boulder in the gully and turned. He started to move some rocks and sand until he uncovered some wooden planks. He pulled the planks up and removed a few more boulders that were beneath them. Then the entrance to the tunnel was revealed. It was just big enough for him to enter. Crispin and Cassian stood at the entrance while others followed Christian inside. When they were twenty feet in, Christian lit a torch. He continued to move forward, and everyone followed him, several of them lighting additional torches. Soon they were three hundred feet in, and to an open area that had a flight of stairs that went up and stopped at a stone wall. Christian found a key on the floor and picked it up. He searched the surface of the wall until he found a crack in the wall. He got one of the pry bars from Edmund and started to pry at the block wall. It moved a little, so Edmund helped him. Soon an opening formed into one of the cells in the dungeon. Christian motioned for everyone to be silent. He stuck his head inside the cell. Others then followed him out of the tunnel into the cell. Christian took the key out of his pocket and opened the cell door. All of them moved silently until they came to another cell door. Christian opened it and found two soldiers sleeping. Edmund came to Christian's side, and they each stabbed one of the soldiers without making a sound. Christian looked up and saw the horn that was blown to signal when he was to be whipped. Col picked up the horn and wrapped it up while Christian walked along the corridor and shined a light into another cell. Christian said, "Ben, are you there?" An old man started to move; he finally got up and made his way to the cell door. Christian opened the door, and Ben slowly walked out. He started to fall, but Christian caught him and laid him softly on the straw-covered floor.

Ben looked at him. "You came back." He started to cry. "I am so sorry, Christian. I am so sorry I was afraid to tell you."

Christian asked, "What are you sorry for?"

"It was my fault your parents were killed. I got drunk that night and was talking about your birthmark. Soldiers found out and questioned me. They ended up dunking me in a trough, and I thought I was going to die. I was not strong enough, and I told them about your birth mark. I did not know they were going to kill your family."

Christian looked up and a tear flowed down his cheek. He looked at Ben, "I forgive you." Ben seemed to shrink in size, and a frown developed on his face. Christian said, "I know you did not mean for all that to happen. I am alive thanks to you and God. I am here to free our people, starting with you."

Ben said, "Thanks, Hope. I am glad to see this day. Your dad would be proud." Ben closed his eyes. Christian held him, knowing the old man was dying. Another tear came down his face, "Please be with him, God." Ben did not breathe anymore.

Christian touched Ben on the side of his head. "You were a good man. God, please take him in and forgive him." Christian got up. He was filled with rage. He put on his sword belt.

David looked at Edmund with a big smile and said, "Are you ready to watch?" Christian moved out of the dungeon and through the building. Suddenly, they entered the kitchen area, and Christian saw Carl standing there. Carl froze in horror. Christian said, "Hi, Carl."

Edmund saw Carl too. "Let me take him." But Christian took

a knife out of his pack and threw it at Carl, hitting him in his neck, killing him instantly. Carl fell backward.

Christian looked at Edmund, "If you must, you can cut his face. I have no time for dramatics." Christian pulled his knife out of Carl's neck and wiped the blood from it before he moved forward.

David said, "This is a focused man." They found a few soldiers nearby sleeping and killed them. Once the building was clear, Christian glanced outside through the open window and saw a few soldiers in the street. He called Alec. "Alec, I need you to come here with two bows." When Alec was in position, Christian pointed out the window, "Do you recognize those soldiers standing by the fire?"

Alec replied, "They are loyal to Brutus."

Christian got his bow ready. "I'll get the one on the right. You get the one on the left." As they both started to pull back their bowstrings, he hesitated. "Wait! Look at the wall over there."

Alec replied, "I see him as well."

Christian said, "They must have stationed these men as decoys. Do you see anyone else over there?"

"No, I do not."

Christian stood up. "Watch them." He walked over to Charles and Alexander. "Alexander, find two men and have them put on the gear of these dead soldiers. Charles, I hear you are good with a bow."

Charles replied, "I am good."

Christian motioned for him to follow. "Grab a bow and come with me." They walked over to the window. Christian let Charles look outside "There are three men out there—two by the fire and one over by the building. I will get the one by the building if you can get the one on the right while Alec gets the one on the left."

Charles replied, "I can do that."

Christian said, "I will shoot first and move out of the way. Then both of you shoot." They all got ready, and Christian shot his arrow. He hit his target, and the soldier fell over. Alec and Charles both hit their targets as well, but one of the soldiers remained standing and started to make sounds. Christian ran out the door with his bow in his hand. Charles followed him while Alec shot another arrow at the standing soldier and then ran outside as well. Christian looked to his right and noticed movement on the roof of a small building. He quickly shot an arrow, and the soldier fell off the roof. Christian ran to the first soldier he had shot, making sure he was dead. As he headed to the other soldier, he looked around and did not see anyone else. Christian grabbed one of the dead soldiers and dragged him into the building. Alec and Charles went out to retrieve the other dead soldier. Christian went back out to get the soldier who had fallen from the roof.

The two men Alexander had found dressed in the soldiers' outfits and took up their gear. Alexander instructed them to take off the soldier gear if they saw their own men. They headed out to the area by the fire. Christian got the men ready. He found Alec, Alexander, Joseph, and Charles. "Brutus has men on the rooftops watching the main wall. I think he planned to sacrifice these two soldiers and have soldiers sound an alarm once one of them fell. When you are walking into position, stay close to the side of the buildings and keep checking the rooftops. If you find soldiers up there, shoot them. Pass this information around."

Charles replied, "I will help you do this." Alec and Joseph instructed their men and left. Alexander left next to inform his men what had just happened. The information was passed to four other teams until Christian, and his team were the last. Christian and his team headed to the two barrack buildings, but Christian did not see any men standing outside. Indeed, he did not see any movement.

Suddenly, a man appeared with his hands up. "Please stop," he shouted. Christian looked around and saw a man standing there. The man said, "Please stop. My son is in there."

Charles said, "I know this man. He is loyal to Brutus."

The man appeared to be nervous. "Brutus took my son and made him a soldier unwillingly. I do not want him to die. The soldiers there are new recruits. Listen, I am not trying to stop you from what you are doing. I just want my son to live."

Christian stepped closer to him. "Tell me where they are then."

The man was shaking. "I do not know where they are. I just know they are not in there." He pointed to the barracks.

Christian thought for a moment. "I think I know where they are. Charles, take four men and watch those doors. I want you to gag this man and tie his hands in front. Have him sit where he was. If he gets up and warns anyone, kill him. If anyone comes out of those doors, do the same as you have done to this guy. If they try to go back inside to warn others, or if they charge you, shoot them. The rest of you will come with me."

Charles replied, "Where are you going?"

Christian looked at him and said, "Too the church." Christian and the men left.

Alec and Joseph made their way along the road. At the end of one road, they saw a two-story house and noticed a platform on the second story with soldiers on it. Alec said, "Any ideas on how we can get up there?"

Joseph looked around and said, "I can get up on this building. I should have a straight shot at them. Station a few men on the other side of the building. If you have a shot at any of the soldiers, take it. When you see a soldier fall, be ready to take the gate." Joseph started to climb as Alec and others got into position closer to the building. When he got to the top of the building, Joseph saw three soldiers on top of the neighboring house. He shot an arrow at the man in the center and then instantly grabbed another arrow and shot it at the man on the left. The first man fell to the ground as the second one turned and saw Joseph, but the arrow knocked him down. Then it became a race between the third man and Joseph. But, out of nowhere, an arrow from below struck the man down. At the same time, Alec and others charged the gates. One man picked up his bow, but Alec killed him with an arrow. Others saw this and surrendered.

Joseph looked at other rooftops and saw one soldier two hundred feet away. He shot an arrow and killed that man. The soldier fell right in front of Crispin who then took care of the castle wall guards. Joseph noticed the castle wall guards were down and signaled Alec. Alec then opened the gates to signal Curtis. Joseph climbed back down to the ground and ran to Alec. "Have you seen any movement from the woods?" he asked.

Alec replied, "I saw a massive shadow move. I believe it was our men.

Joseph looked down the wall and saw other men coming toward them. "Looks like others are about to join us as well from inside." Soon Crispin's team joined them with a captive.

Crispin said, "Look who I have here. It is little William! He and others were forced to be on the wall. If they refused, they and their families would be killed. It seems they wanted Christian to have them killed so the people would turn on him."

Joseph asked William, "Do you know where the soldiers are?"

William looked out at the huts, "There are men scattered in some of those huts outside and at the chapel."

Crispin said, "I'm going to take half of my men with me to find Christian. The rest will stay with you just in case something happens. I see more men are coming from the inside, and it appears that Curtis is nearly here as well."

Joseph replied, "I hope they're quite enough. Go and tell Christian. I will send others your way."

Crispin left with a small contingent of men.

By this, time Christian, Cassian, Col, and David had made it to the chapel. Christian noticed two men standing in front and another three on the chapel steeple. David saw this too. "What is your plan now, Christian?"

Christian looked around and said, "I know those people in that house. Cassian, if I get you in place on the second floor, do you think you and some men would be able to kill the soldiers in the steeple and keep anyone from climbing back up there?"

Cassian looked up. "It can be done."

Christian said, "David and Col, stay here with these men. More should be coming soon. I am going to the owners of this house to talk to them."

Christian approached the house with Cassian and a few other men. He opened the door cautiously and went quietly upstairs. He found the couple sleeping and walked over to the man. He put his hand slightly on the man's mouth and said, "This is Christian. Do not be startled." The man opened his eyes and said, "I cannot see you, but I recognize your voice. You have come, my boy. Your dad would be proud of you." His wife woke up and was startled, but her husband quieted her down.

Christian said, "I have some men with me. We need to take care of those soldiers in the steeple. Can you tell me how many are inside and where others might be?"

The man replied, "There are about thirty inside the chapel. I believe the rest are at the castle. You have Brutus worried. Carl has been hiding as well."

Christian said with no concern, "Carl is dead."

The man looked at Christian. "Yes. Use the windows."

Christian replied, "I must leave, but these three men are going to use the windows."

The man replied, "May God be with you."

Christian said, "Shoot after you see the first man fall from in front of the doors. Edmund, get into position with your men." Christian then left.

By then, Curtis had arrived with the other men and women. They had all made it inside the castle grounds without waking anyone. Once they got in, Joseph secured the gates. Curtis looked at one of the captives. "They made little William join. They must not have many men."

Joseph replied, "Little William informed us that there are some of Brutus's soldiers out there in the huts. Others are in the chapel. I sent men that way."

Curtis replied, "I will join them with these men." He turned to them. "Follow me."

When Christian returned to where Col and David were, he was joined by Crispin and fifteen other men. Christian said, "I was told there are thirty men in that building. There are only two entrances, and we are going to secure them. There might be a soldier in front of the other entrance. Crispin, take this rope and secure the side door with it. When I kill the first guard, Cassian and the others will take care of the ones in the steeple. I am going to secure the main entrance with those poleaxes. He pointed to a pile of military equipment. If anyone makes it out the doors or tries to get out a window, kill him. After we secure this building, I am going to head to the castle. I want you to take ten men and secure that side. Stay out of the light and find cover if you can."

Christian looked down the road and saw more men coming with Curtis leading the way. He sent Col to tell them to slow down and tell them about the guards outside of the chapel. Christian sent five men to go to the back of the building to watch the windows. Soon Curtis arrived with the extra men.

Curtis was ready to fight. "What do you want us to do?"

Christian replied, "Send ten men to cover the side windows. If anyone tries to come out, kill them. Send five more to help cover the side entrance door. Once they are in position, we will start this and then secure the doors. Once I shoot an arrow, I want you to bring twenty men and cover the front entrance just in case someone does get out. I'm going to head to the castle. Remember, we need to watch the castle balcony."

Soon everyone was in position. Christian looked at Edmund and said, "You take the one on the right. I'll get the one on the left." They slowly got into position so they could shoot the soldiers in the front entrance. They both hit their targets, the soldiers falling to their deaths. Cassian and his men shot their arrows, and the men were killed, but when they fell, the church bells began to ring! Christian ran as fast as he could to the front entrance. He grabbed the poleaxes and shoved them through the door handles. He grabbed the fallen men's swords and shoved them through the handles as well to keep the doors secured. Then he darted back to where he had been in position.

Soon soldiers were trying to get out of the church, but they were unsuccessful. Some tried to get out through the windows, but they were killed instantly. Some tried to make it to the steeple, but they were also killed by arrows. Curtis had his men in position. Christian said to him, "I'm going to head to the castle and finish this. I want you to take control of this. No one leaves that building till this is done."

Christian grabbed a few other men and left the area. The chapel bells continued to ring. Christian looked back at the church. The sound of the bells had warned Brutus that something was not right. The surprise was now gone. Christian's only hope was that Brutus had not had enough time to prepare for his arrival.

David looked at Christian. "Well, now it's going to get interesting. They are going to be ready at the castle." Col took out the horn and blew it steadily. The sound awakened people who jumped up and looked outside. They saw armed men and women running by them. The newcomers were not wearing soldiers' gear, and they seemed to have grabbed whatever they could use as weapons. Col ran around the buildings blowing the horn. This encouraged more and more people to come out. They all remembered the horn being blown when Christian was being led to be whipped.

A group of Brutus's soldiers came out of hiding in the huts and ran to the gates. Soon they were killed by arrows. At the chapel, the captives managed to get through one of the front doors, but as soon as they got out, they fell to their deaths at the hands of the archers. Ten charged the door, but all died in an instant. After this happened, the remaining captives stopped trying to get out. Instead, they raised a white cloth to surrender.

Christian and his men were shielded by the last building that could provide cover. Beyond the building was an open courtyard in front of the castle. Christian stopped everyone. He looked around at the building and could see men on the balcony and on the main level with bows. Christian noticed that Brutus's men did not have cover. Brutus must not have thought Christian and his men would ever get that far.

Christian saw more people coming out to join him, but he was concerned they would get killed by arrows. He looked at the buildings and noticed the roofs were vertical peak to the front entrances and balconies of the castle. He sent thirty people to a position on two roofs and made sure they had extra arrows. Christian had other people position themselves on the ground. They too were supplied with arrows. He knew it would be a massacre if people charged right at them. He removed one of the doors from one of the houses and used his sword to make a few notches. He found a rope and tied it around the door, securing it in the notches, creating a large shield. Edmund and David followed his example and soon had shields of their own. Christian looked at Edmund and David and said, "It must be done."

Edmund ordered his men to start shooting arrows. He went to one house and approached Brutus's soldiers at an angle. He thought that he could just keep moving forward at an angle until he hugged the castle wall. Brutus's men started shooting at him. Christian's people continued to shoot arrows at them. A few of the soldiers on the balcony fell to their deaths while others stayed hidden behind the wall. The soldiers on the main level outside hid behind a barricade, and still one by one, they collapsed to their maker.

Christian continued to make his way forward. Soon he was halfway through the courtyard. He looked back and saw two others following him doing the same. Christian's men kept on shooting arrows at Brutus's soldiers. Finally, Christian reached the paving stones and took out his sword. He continued hugging the wall and started striking the soldiers using the door as a shield. Arrows were still flying both ways. Edmund and David reached Christian and started attacking Brutus's men. Soon more people charged Brutus's soldiers, and more succumbed to their deaths. Christian dropped his long sword and grabbed a long knife from the harness on his back. He dropped the door and struck a soldier who was positioned in front of him. With his left hand, he grabbed the other long knife and killed a few more of Brutus's men. Edmund and David dropped their doors and started attacking as well.

Soon Col had more people with him fighting as it continued in the castle. One of Brutus's soldiers was about to stab David, but Christian stopped him. David saw this and kept on fighting. While the fighting was going on, Brutus appeared on the main floor, but he quickly left in desperation. Christian's men and the castle villagers were overtaking Brutus's soldiers. Soon, the remaining defeated soldiers dropped their swords.

Christian ran up the stairs after Brutus. Col and David noticed this and started to follow him. Brutus tried to escape to his room, but Christian was right behind him. Before he could close the door, Brutus turned around and saw Christian. Brutus knew his death was imminent, but he addressed his enemy in a cocky manner. "So, you think you won. You know who is coming for you, don't you? I just sent someone to let him know what has happened here." Christian just looked at him, and Brutus continued, "So you have your two long knives. You sure are a Christian, aren't you?"

Christian replied, "I don't want to have to kill you.'"

As Brutus had been talking, he had been walking backward slowly. At the same time, Christian had been advancing, closing the distance between them. Brutus said, "You want me to fall to my death like King William did. That is not going to happen."

Christian replied, "Why do you not drop your sword and surrender? I do not want to have to kill you."

Brutus responded, "You want to take pity on me. How merciful you are. All those people are going to die because of you."

Christian stood his ground boldly "I will see that does not happen, but I will need all the help from God because I cannot do it alone."

Brutus chuckled. "More God stuff—after all the killing you have done tonight?"

Christian glared at him as if he was looking right into Brutus's soul. "I did not want any of it, but the only way to stop people like you is with violence. I know you were not just going to walk away."

Brutus was getting close to the edge of the balcony. "If you drop your knives, I will drop mine."

Christian paused because he was tired of death. He dropped his long knives. Brutus, standing firmly on the balcony, raised his sword. "You fool!" he shouted! He moved forward to charge Christian, but an arrow from somewhere outside struck him. Brutus collapsed onto the floor murmuring, "He is coming. He is coming." But then he closed his eyes and spoke no more.

David and Cole stepped into the room. They had seen what had happened. Col asked, "Who is coming here? Who did he send for?" He was becoming anxious.

David remained calm. He picked up one of Christian's long knives and held it up. He got down on one knee and said, "You are a man I can follow and call my king."

Remember to love God. God Love us.
Christian

Printed in the USA
CPSIA information can be obtained
at www.ICGtesting.com
LVHW091150081124
795950LV00003B/360

* 9 7 9 8 3 8 5 0 2 6 6 6 1 *